To

_____

With Love From

_____

A Mother's Love

Santa Montefiore

A Mother's Love

**SIMON &
SCHUSTER**

London · New York · Sydney · Toronto · New Delhi

A CBS COMPANY

First published in ebook in Great Britain by Simon & Schuster UK Ltd, 2013
A CBS COMPANY

This hardback edition 2016

A Mother's Love Copyright © Santa Montefiore, 2013
Songs of Love and War excerpt © Santa Montefiore, 2015

1 3 5 7 9 10 8 6 4 2

Simon & Schuster UK Ltd
1st Floor
222 Gray's Inn Road
London WC1X 8HB

www.simonandschuster.co.uk

Simon & Schuster Australia, Sydney
Simon & Schuster India, New Delhi

A CIP catalogue record for this book
is available from the British Library

HB ISBN: 978-1-4711-4660-2
Ebook ISBN 978-1-4711-2860-8

This book is a work of fiction. Names, characters, places and
incidents are either a product of the author's imagination or are
used fictitiously. Any resemblance to actual people, living or
dead, events or locales, is entirely coincidental.

Typeset by M Rules
Printed and bound by CPI Group (UK) Ltd, Croydon, CR0 4YY

Simon & Schuster UK Ltd are committed to sourcing paper
that is made from wood grown in sustainable forests and supports the Forest
Stewardship Council, the leading international forest certification organisation.
Our books displaying the FSC logo are printed on FSC certified paper.

To mothers everywhere

Dear Reader,

A mother's love for her child is a unique kind of magic. There is no love stronger or more enduring. Nothing can give so much pleasure and yet cause so much pain. I often say to my children that I would love them whatever they did, and I truly believe I would. I might not like what they do, but I will never stop loving them. I can't.

When I wrote my first novel I had only just met my future husband. Children were far from my thoughts and I could only guess at the way a mother loves her children by observing the way my own mother loved us.

I was certain in the knowledge that she loved us unconditionally. She always put us first and was always patient and kind and understanding. She was my best friend and still is. I would call her from boarding school about the silliest things and she'd listen and advise and I never felt that I was boring her. To the contrary, everything about my life seemed to interest her, however trivial. I knew that I could turn to her in times of need and that she'd always be there. I could count on her and that's a wonderful thing in a mother.

*Of course, on a practical level she was very
efficient and generous with her time. She cooked our
favourite meals when we came home from school. I
even came home on weekends from university with
bags of dirty clothes and she'd wash and iron them
and have them all piled up neatly in the hall ready
for my departure on the Sunday. When I moved into
my first flat in London she went through the attic and
drove lamps, throws, cushions and bedspreads up from
Hampshire to make the place more homely.*

*I remember dressing to go to a party and
wandering into her bedroom in my ball gown. She
stood in front of the mirror, looking elegant in a
caramel-coloured strapless dress with a stunning
necklace around her neck, and she turned to me
and narrowed her eyes. 'This would look better on
you,' she said, taking off her necklace. It didn't look
better on me, as it happened, but she always put my
needs above her own. 'I've already got my man,'
she laughed. The truth was that she would sacrifice
anything for us. She would have given me her dress
if she had felt I'd dazzle in it. I appreciated her,
of course I did, but it wasn't until I had my own*

*children that I understood the might of that love. Now
I find myself doing the same for my daughter and I
smile as I hear myself repeating my mother's words:
'Really, Lily, this will look better on you!'*

*My novels deal with love on every level.
Romantic love is only one aspect of the many faces
of love. There is love for one's friends, one's family
and one's pets, and they are all fascinating to me.
I think we all know, deep in our hearts, that love
is the only thing that matters in our lives. Material
things won't hold any value once we are gone. I
know that when I leave this world I won't care how
many books reached the bestsellers lists, I'll care
about how many people I touched in a positive way
through my actions and my work. I'll care about
the people I love and who love me and I'll still
want them to know, as I do now, that love binds us
forever. Death cannot sever it. That's what inspired*
A Mother's Love.

*I have always had a strong sense of the Afterlife.
I know our existence does not end with physical
death. I have seen spirits all through my life, which
I consider a great privilege, and I don't doubt that*

those we love and lose are always with us, just beyond the limits of our perception. Therefore, in my novels, death is just another side of life. It's not an end but a continuation of existence; a comma on the endless road that is eternity.

Since having my own children, who are now thirteen and fifteen, I have learned much about love. I have learned that the greatest pleasure of all comes from watching my children enjoying themselves. Their happiness is more fulfilling than any material pleasure could ever be. I have also learned that their pain is more excruciating for me than any pain I might suffer myself. Most crucially I have learned what it feels like to love someone more than I love myself.

Relationships are complicated. Nothing is straight forward. Life is a training ground, my father used to tell me wisely. We're here to learn about one thing and one thing only: love. Sounds simple, but when we look at our own lives we realise that the hardest things we have to learn are all aspects of love: forgiveness, acceptance, understanding, tolerance, kindness, compassion, patience, gratitude and selflessness. Happiness can only come from love however much the media tells you otherwise – and sometimes it takes terrible loss and tragedy to teach us its value.

Mother's Day is a celebration but also a day of thanks. Mothers on the whole are selfless and hard-working women – the saying 'A woman's work is never done' is absolutely true. It's as exhausting as it is rewarding! Raising children is probably the most meaningful job a woman will ever do. The importance of teaching children values and independence so that they can one day go out into the world and make a contribution to society cannot be underestimated. A day of gratitude is a small way of thanking mothers whose love is often overlooked or underappreciated. But that's the funny thing about mothers – they love their children without expecting anything in return.

I hope you enjoy this small book. I hope the story touches you but also that it makes you wonder at the strength and power of your love. I hope it opens the minds of children to the selfless love that their mothers have for them. Most of all I hope that those who have suffered loss know that love never dies. Ever.

With love and gratitude to all my readers,

Santa Montefiore

Chapter 1

Robert strode purposefully through the orchard to his mother's house, accompanied by his loyal golden Labrador, Tarquin. The evening light had softened to a warm honey tone as the sun sank behind the fields, turning the sky pink. The air was thick with the sweet scents of mown grass and ripening wheat and the ground was already dampening with dew. Pigeons billed and cooed in the lime trees as they settled down to roost and a pair of fluffy blue tits squabbled playfully about the bird feeder his wife Celeste had hung from a pear tree in the no-man's-land between their modest farmhouse and his parents' much grander home further down the valley. From there he could see the tiled rooftops of their seventeenth-century manor, mottled with moss and algae and weathered to a muted reddish brown. The rows of ornate-shafted chimneys seemed to balance precariously above the triangular gables like unsteady sentinels, weary of keeping watch. One, which was no longer in use, was now the nest of an uncommonly large pigeon who had settled in for the summer. The manor had the tousled charm of a much-beloved toy whose fur has worn away in places because of so much affection, and Robert felt a surge of fondness for the house that would always be home.

Robert had grown up at Chawton Grange with his three sisters, but he was the only child to remain as the girls had since married and moved away. He loved the farm and had fond memories of driving tractors in his youth and helping out at harvest time during the long summer holidays. Growing up had been easy in such a beautiful place. Now, as life grew more complicated, he reflected on those long, lazy days in the fields, where grief had not yet sought him out and the future had stretched ahead like a pure summer sky, clear and optimistic. He could never have foreseen how things would change.

Robert had lost his eight-year-old son Jack to leukaemia sixteen months before. He would never get over it, but he had learned to live with it, like the dull, throbbing pain of a chronic condition that never goes away. He often wondered whether his loss was in some perverse way life's balancing of the books, payment for thirty years of unadulterated pleasure. Had he been asked, he would happily have chosen thirty years of misery in exchange for his son's good health. Celeste had not yet learned to live with her grief. It had gushed and flowed around her like a terrible flood of pain, forming an impassable moat, hemming her in and forcing him out. She had shrunk into herself like a tortoise resentful of the light. Her laughter no longer bubbled and her smile had ceased altogether so that her face had set into a taut, unhappy scowl. He had not only lost his child, but he had lost his wife, too. Jack had taken her heart with him, leaving his father with nothing but the shell.

He thrust his hands into his pockets and walked out of the orchard into his parents' garden. The sight of home momentarily uplifted him, like ascending out of shade into sunshine. Every corner of that serene oasis echoed with the laughter of his childhood games. Now that laughter reached him in waves of nostalgia and his heart ached for that innocence, now gone, and that ignorance, so sweet, because back then he hadn't known the bitter taste of bereavement. Back then he hadn't known the ferocity of love, either.

His father, Huxley, was busy up a ladder, deadheading the roses in a panama hat and pale linen jacket, while his mother sat on the terrace in regal splendour, a cigarette in one hand, a biro in the other, her large dogs at her feet and a half-eaten box of chocolate truffles on the table in front of her, doing the crossword.

She sensed his approach and popped a truffle into her mouth. 'I thought it wouldn't be long before you trotted down to reproach me,' she said, putting the newspaper aside with a sigh. Robert descended the stone steps onto the terrace.

'Help yourself to a glass of wine,' suggested his father from the ladder. 'It's that Chilean Sauvignon Blanc you gave me to try. I think it's rather good. Has a fruity taste.'

'Listen, Mum, why can't *you* have him?' Robert

poured himself a glass and sat on the bench opposite his mother. 'You *are* his grandmother.'

Marigold took off her glasses and fixed him with pale, turquoise eyes. At seventy-three those eyes still had the power to mesmerize, even though her body, which had expanded over the years like a sponge in water, retained none of its once infamous allure. Wrapped in layers of loose cottons and fine pashmina wraps, Marigold had given in to the chocolates and cakes she had spent her youth avoiding, and her long blonde hair was pinned loosely on top of her head so that it resembled the pigeon's nest on the chimney. 'Because I'm very busy,' she said briskly, lifting her chin.

Robert stared at her – the least busy woman in the south of England – and pulled a bewildered face. 'Busy? Doing what?'

'I'm afraid I simply can't entertain an eight-year-old boy for five days. I have people coming and Mrs Cleaves will be on holiday so I'll have to cook, which you know I loathe. I'm going up to London midweek, Freddie and Ginny have asked us to the opera, and I've decided to learn bridge, so I'm joining a club in Alresford. You see, no time to look after a small boy.'

She averted her eyes and took a sip of wine, which immediately made her look shifty.

Robert knew his mother had deliberately arranged things to avoid having his sister's child for a week, but he couldn't work out why. It was very out of character for her to be selfish. When Jack had been alive he and Celeste had resorted to inventing things in order to keep her *away*, and she had jumped at any opportunity to have him to herself. 'There must be somebody else she can leave him with?' he suggested in desperation, picturing Celeste sobbing on her bed at the prospect of having a child in the house again when her emotions were still so raw. 'Please, Mum. Celeste is beside herself.'

Marigold's blue eyes softened with compassion. 'Darling, they're moving back from Australia after having been away for sixteen years. Georgia has no friends here any more, only us. She wouldn't have asked you if she hadn't been desperate. You're her last resort. It's only five days. I think you'll manage.'

'It's not me I'm worried about. I have no problem with looking after my nephew. I'm thinking about Celeste.'

'Georgia says he's a very easy child. He just entertains himself. He won't need much looking after, he's very independent. That's what happens when you have older sisters. You were always independent, too.'

'God,' he groaned. 'I promised Celeste I'd sort it out.'

Marigold popped another chocolate into her mouth and patted one of the Alsatians which was now sitting up and demanding attention. She shrugged. '*Tant pis*, darling. Such is life. You might find it turns out to be a blessing.'

Robert drained his glass then made his way back to the cottage with Tarquin, leaving the warmth of his parents' garden for the chill of his own. When he was growing up the cottage had been inhabited by the farm manager, but as soon as Celeste had got pregnant his father had handed it over to him. The manager had been an expert rose grower, and when Celeste had moved in she had lovingly tended them, but since Jack had died she hadn't touched them, so that now few buds flowered and all one could see was a tangle of thorny tentacles falling away from the twine that once held them against the walls.

When he reached the cottage he found his wife at her bedroom window, staring out over the field towards the woods, as if she longed to run there and never come back. As she heard him coming up the stairs she swung round. 'So, what did she say?' Her face was contorted with anxiety.

He shook his head. 'She can't.'

'Can't?'

'I'm sorry, darling. The child is coming to stay. There's nothing I can do.'

Celeste was speechless. She put a frail white hand to her mouth, where the fingers trembled against her lips, and tears trickled down her cheeks. Robert sighed heavily and attempted to embrace her, but she stopped him, shaking her head vigorously. Her eyes spoke of her resentment, as if it was all his fault, so he turned and left her alone, as he so often did now, his own heart brimming with bitterness because Jack was his son, too. But Celeste couldn't see past her own grief to notice his.

Celeste sat on the bed and turned her eyes once again to the woods. The wheat shimmered in the breeze like a golden sea as darkness crept up slowly, swallowing the remains of the light and another day. For that she was grateful; one less to live without Jack.

In a strange way Celeste had settled into her grief. Even though it was painful, there was comfort in its familiar patterns. She was used to the dead feeling in her soul, the chill of winter that had taken all colour and joy from her spirit; the bleak, flat light, as hard as slate, which had pervaded her world. The prospect of having another child in the house had suddenly disrupted her rhythm and wrenched her out of herself. How would she cope? What would she do with him? How could Robert have allowed this to happen?

Chapter 2

The morning of Bruno's arrival Celeste refused to get out of bed. Robert had taken the day off, leaving his young employee Jacques-Louis to manage the wine shop, so that he could welcome his nephew and say hello to his sister, whom he hadn't seen since she'd flown over for Jack's funeral. Marigold and Huxley had driven round and now waited in the kitchen with cups of tea and biscuits. The atmosphere was tense, especially as Celeste had not yet emerged. Tarquin sighed from his basket, closed his eyes and went back to sleep. The sound of rain on the window panes only added to the dreary mood inside.

At last Celeste appeared in the doorway, a stiff and distant creature. She had tied her hair back into a severe ponytail and folded her arms across her chest in an obvious display of defensiveness. She could not disguise her fury and barely greeted her mother-in-law, who bit into another biscuit out of nervousness. Only Huxley chatted away in his usual jovial manner, as if nothing were untoward. 'I took the dogs up to Tin Sheds this morning and d'you know what I saw? There in the middle of the field was a family of deer. Wonderful sight in spite of the damage they do to the crops.'

'You should get your gun out, Dad,' Robert suggested.

'I've grown magnanimous in my old age, Robert. What with the hares and rabbits, this farm is a haven for wildlife and I rather like it that way, although they eat away all my profits. It's a losing battle and I've accepted I've lost.'

Tarquin's ears pricked before anyone else heard the car. A moment later the rumble of the engine defused the awkwardness of waiting but seemed to suck the oxygen out of the room. Celeste's shoulders tensed, Robert paled, Marigold caught her husband's eye.

But Huxley clapped his big hands and beamed. 'Ah, good,' he said. 'Robert, go and fetch an umbrella so they don't get soaked.' Tarquin stood by the door, wagging his tail, until Robert appeared with a golfing umbrella to open it. They dashed outside together.

Marigold didn't dare look at Celeste. She could see her taut profile out of the corner of her eye and feel her resentment as if the air around her were charged with prickly little filaments. She might have buckled then, if she hadn't thought of her son and the children he longed for but wasn't allowed to have. Instead, she lifted her chin and stepped forward as her daughter and grandson hurried up the path beneath Robert's umbrella, bursting into the hall with peals of laughter.

'Goodness, I forgot how much it rains in England!' Georgia exclaimed happily. 'Oh, Daddy, it's so good to see you!' She embraced her father, pressing her cold face to his cheek. 'You've lost weight!' she said, turning on her mother. 'You have been feeding him, haven't you, Mum?'

'Darling, he's just getting old,' Marigold chuckled, gathering her daughter into her arms like a fat hen. 'You look well, though. Gosh, it's good to have you back. Now where's my grandson? Bruno?'

The boy stood behind his mother in a pair of jeans and trainers, his thick brown hair falling over eyes the colour of Marigold's milk chocolate truffles. He smiled diffidently, a little overwhelmed by the strange faces staring at him. Shyly, he put out his hand.

Marigold smiled affectionately. 'Goodness, you *are* polite,' she said. 'But I'm your grandmother, so I'm going to give you a jolly good hug.' The child caught his uncle's eye as he was enveloped in cotton and cashmere and his grandmother's lily of the valley perfume.

Robert pulled a face, at which Bruno grinned back, his cheeks flushing the colour of strawberries. 'Mum, do put him down. Boys hate to be mollycoddled!' he said.

'Oh darling, you're so grown up!' she gushed, releasing him. 'I can hardly believe it. How lucky we are that you've come to stay.' Then, remembering her daughter-in-law, she swung around. 'You've never met your aunt Celeste, have you? Well, here she is. Celeste?'

Marigold tried to disguise her anxiety with a chuckle, but her chest felt tight with dread. She watched her daughter-in-law shake the child's hand and manage a wan smile, and longed for her to muster up a little more enthusiasm, if only to make the boy feel welcome. She was relieved when Robert stepped in and introduced him to Tarquin. The child's face opened with pleasure at the sight of the dog. He stroked his wet head and laughed as the animal lifted his nose and tried to lick his hand. 'He's awesome,' he said. 'I think Tarquin and I are going to be buddies.'

'I think you are, too,' Marigold interjected.

'Do you like tractors, Bruno?' his grandfather asked.

'Sure,' Bruno replied with a shrug.

'I'll show you around the farm and you can drive one, if you like.'

'Really? Drive one?' The boy's eyes shone excitedly. He glanced at his mother.

Georgia put up her hands. 'I don't want to know what you two get up to,' she laughed. 'Celeste, I'm leaving him in your capable hands.'

Celeste managed another weak smile. 'Don't worry, I'll look after him,' she said softly. 'Bruno, would you like to see your room?' The child nodded. They set off up the stairs, followed by Tarquin.

Marigold seized her daughter's arm. 'I hope he's going to be all right,' she hissed.

'Mum, he's going to be fine. He loves the countryside and he adores his uncle Robert. They really clicked when he came to Sydney. Don't worry about him. He's got a wisdom beyond his years. Trust me, I wouldn't have agreed to leave him here if I didn't think he could handle it.'

Marigold sighed. 'Well, we're just through the garden if he wants to come down.'

Georgia smiled and patted her mother's arm. 'I know. He'll seek you out if he needs you.'

Celeste showed Bruno the spare room. It was at the end of the corridor with a big window that looked out over the garden. They could see the chimneys of Chawton Grange through the rain. 'Shame the weather's so bad,' said Celeste, struggling to find something to say. Her instinct was to reject this child who had stepped in to take Jack's place in the house, but her head reminded her of his innocence. He was a boy, after all. Just a boy who had no idea of the unhappiness he was causing.

'Oh, I love the rain,' Bruno replied. 'I like to stand in it under an umbrella. I like the sound.'

'Really? I hate getting wet,' said Celeste, folding her arms across her chest.

'Tarquin doesn't mind that, do you, Tarquin?' He patted the dog's head again.

'Did you have a dog in Sydney?'

'No, I had a rabbit. But they don't do much.'

'Dogs make better friends,' Celeste added, realizing as she spoke just how much of a comfort Tarquin had been to her since she lost Jack. 'Are you hungry? What do you like to eat?'

'Not really,' he replied. 'I don't like beans.'

'I don't like Brussels sprouts.'

'Mum makes me eat them.'

'I won't.'

Bruno grinned. 'That's good.'

'While you're here, you can do pretty much anything you like.' She hoped he would entertain himself. She had no intention of spending any more time with him than absolutely necessary.

When they returned downstairs, Robert had brought in Bruno's case, his gumboots and coat, and Georgia was sitting at the kitchen table with her parents, drinking a cup of tea. 'You're so good to have him, Celeste. I can't tell you how much I appreciate it.'

Celeste suppressed the urge to snap at Georgia, and instead asked, 'What sort of things does he like to do?'

'Oh, anything, he's not fussy.'

'Robert will be working, but I suppose I'll find things for him to do.'

'He likes Lego, colouring, exploring. There's plenty to do outside. It'll take him five days to explore the grounds here. He's pretty happy on his own.'

Celeste nodded. 'He can use the playroom.' Her face blanched further as her thoughts turned to Jack's old room of toys. She averted her eyes. 'I've got lots of Lego.'

'He'll love that.'

'And I'll kick a football at him when I'm home,' Robert interjected enthusiastically.

'He likes footie. His dad has trained him to be a pretty good goalie.'

'When's Mark joining you?' Robert asked.

'He's bringing the girls over in a couple of weeks. I'll have everything sorted by then.'

'It'll be so nice to have you in the same country for a change,' said Marigold happily.

'Tell me about it. I've missed you all so much!'

'It's about time Bruno got to know his family,' said Huxley. 'And learned to speak English,' he added firmly.

'Oh darling, you sound just like your father, Grandpa Hartley,' Marigold scolded. 'Old Hartley fought in the war and hated anything foreign. His idea of speaking a foreign language was to talk in English very loudly.'

'He'll lose his Australian accent soon enough,' Georgia reassured him.

Huxley nodded. 'Good. We'll do all we can to accelerate the process.'

Once everyone had gone, Celeste showed Bruno the playroom. It had remained untouched for almost a year and a half. Boxes of Lego, trains and plastic guns were placed in neat rows against one wall, a table and chairs against another with a container filled with pens and crayons and a rattan basket of plain paper. A big red sofa dominated the room and an open fireplace stood empty and desolate. There was a large flat-screen television and lots of DVDs of all Jack's favourite movies lined up in the bookcase. Celeste switched on the lights and the room seemed to spring to life. The little boy wasted no time in pulling out the boxes and rummaging through them. He quickly lost himself in his endeavour and Celeste had to swallow back her tears, because Jack had sat on the rug just like Bruno. She turned away, for the sight was too painful. It was all she could do to restrain herself from asking him to leave her son's toys alone. This had been Jack's room. She wasn't sure she was ready to share it with another child. But she had no choice. She had been forced to welcome this usurper. Didn't anyone understand her pain?

Chapter 3

Robert was in his study when Celeste came looking for him. He saw her in the doorway and stopped what he was doing. She folded her arms and sighed. 'Are you OK?' he asked, weary of always being the one to reach out.

She nodded. 'He's in the playroom.'

'Are you OK with that?'

She shrugged. 'I have no choice. It's hard to see a child in there again.'

'He's found things to play with?'

'Jack's things.' She frowned, fighting the impulse to snatch them back and guard them, like she had snatched and guarded her son's memory.

'Good.'

She turned away, then hesitated and pursed her lips. 'Robert, he's the same age as Jack was.'

'I know.'

'I mean, I knew, I suppose, I just hadn't thought . . . that he'd remind me so much of him.'

Upstairs she set about unpacking Bruno's clothes. The rain had now stopped and the sun was peeping through the cloud, shining brightly onto the glittering countryside. She opened the drawers of the dresser and placed Bruno's T-shirts and sweaters in neat piles. As she did so she felt a satisfactory sense of purpose. She took her time, making sure everything was in its place. Slippers beside the bed, dressing gown on the hook behind the door, toothbrush and paste in the bathroom.

She realized then just how bored she'd been. In the days before Jack got sick she had run her own business making embroidered quilts and bedlinen. She had been quite successful, especially at making children's quilts. They were all tailored to each child, the squares embroidered with their favourite things in their favourite colours. In the beginning word had been spread by satisfied clients, but then she had set up an e-commerce site on the Internet and she'd struggled to meet the demand. Then Jack got sick and she didn't have the time or the will to keep going. The Swedish-style house that Robert had had built for her business at the bottom of the garden had been locked for three years now. She hadn't set foot in there, although in the past it had been her sanctuary and one of her greatest pleasures. Jack had sat on the floor and set out all the cotton reels in order of colour. There had been over sixty different shades and he had loved the challenge. Sometimes, when she had been under pressure to finish a quilt, he had brought his homework in after school or sat at the table colouring while she worked. The memory of his little face, so full of concentration, caused her battered heart to groan. She tore herself away from the past and pushed Bruno's case under the bed.

She set about making lunch. Roast chicken, because all children like chicken. She could hear Bruno talking to himself as he played. If she hadn't known better she might have thought he had company. At lunch he chatted away as if he had known his uncle and aunt forever. He was uninhibited and curious and seemed older than his years. She couldn't remember Jack being so articulate and confident. After lunch

Robert played football with him in the garden, making a goal out of sticks, then they set off to explore the farm together with Grandpa Huxley, the big Alsatians and Tarquin.

Celeste went into the playroom to tidy away the toys. She shed tears onto the Lego, spending an excessive amount of time putting the pieces into the box. It was unbearable to think that Jack was never coming back. She could sort out his toys and place the boxes neatly on the shelves again, but he'd never return to play with them.

The sun began to set, flooding the gardens with a soft amber light and her heart with melancholy. The scents rose up from the borders and the clamour of birds grew louder as they squabbled for places to roost. At last the rumble of Robert's car could be heard coming along the farm track and Celeste felt her heart contract with dread.

She walked round to the front of the house. Bruno jumped out of the car, breathless with excitement. 'I drove a tractor!' he exclaimed, hurrying up the path with Tarquin at his heels. 'I climbed on the grain and Uncle Robert chased me. Then he lost his shoe.' The child laughed with such abandon that Celeste found herself chuckling with him. She almost resented him for making her smile, for she had grown used to her misery and had found refuge in the dark comfort of her unhappiness. 'We searched and searched for it and then Tarquin found it. Isn't he clever? It was hidden in the grain. Grandpa let me sit in a combine and says that when they cut again I can ride in it. The rain has made it all wet so they won't be cutting until it's dry. I hope it doesn't rain again so I can go on the combine. It's awesome!'

'You must be hungry,' she said. 'Do you want some tea?'

'Yes please.'

'Come on, then. I'll find something to fill you up.' Before she turned to go into the house she saw Robert coming up the path towards her.

He shook his head and grinned. 'That child has a lot of energy!'

'He's had a lovely time.'

'And worn me and Dad out!'

'You'll be relieved to go back to work tomorrow.' She felt her resentment cloud the fleeting sense of joy she had just experienced. Tomorrow she'd be alone with Bruno. What then?

Robert put his hand in the small of her back and led her into the cottage. 'No, I won't,' he said. 'I'd much rather be here.'

She fed Bruno fish fingers and ran him a bath. Afraid to leave him in the water on his own, she pottered about tidying the already immaculate sink and cupboard beneath. He chatted blithely, lolling in the warm water. She kept herself busy so she didn't have to look at him. She resisted slipping into the old routine she had enjoyed with Jack, of washing his face and soaping his hands and feet, because she knew it would only make her cry. She didn't want to cry in front of Bruno.

After the bath he pulled on his spaceship pyjamas and she put him to bed. She tucked him in and watched him snuggle against his bear. Hovering by the door, she didn't know whether to kiss him goodnight, or read him a story. She definitely sensed that she was lacking somehow and that he sensed it too, because he looked at her with his big brown eyes and in them she recognized anxiety.

'Sleep well,' she said.

'Yes,' he replied, suddenly diffident. Not the same little boy who had been talking so contentedly in the bath. He seemed smaller now and a little forlorn.

'If you need us, we're just down the corridor.' He nodded. 'I'll send Robert up to say goodnight.'

But Robert was already coming along the corridor with Tarquin. She watched them walk past her. The child's face blossomed into a smile and he sat up. 'He's come to say goodnight to you,' Robert said.

Bruno leant over to pat him. 'Where does he sleep?'

'In the kitchen in his basket.'

'Isn't he lonely on his own?'

'No. You don't get lonely on your own, do you?'

'But I'm not alone. I have Brodie.'

Robert laughed. 'And he's a very fine bear.'

'If Tarquin gets lonely he can come and sleep with me.'

'Then you wouldn't sleep a wink, would you? Now, bedtime.' The child's eyes were no longer dark with anxiety. He lay down contentedly and Robert drew up the bedclothes so that all Celeste could see was the boy's rich brown hair peeping out of the top.

Her husband bent down and kissed his forehead. 'God bless,' he said and patted the bedclothes.

Celeste turned away and went downstairs. She didn't want to feel moved by the sight of Robert kissing his little nephew. She held onto her resentment, fearing that if she let it go, she'd have nothing left. Robert joined her in the kitchen and poured them both a glass of wine. Then he went to the sitting room and turned on the television. She knew he did that to avoid talking to her. She wasn't good company these days. Once they had been eager to share their day; now she was eager to end it.

But a little boy was sleeping upstairs and he had changed everything. They were no longer alone. The house vibrated with the child's presence as if a fire had been lit against her will, infusing the familiar cold with a new warmth. She cooked spaghetti and they ate it in front of the television. Celeste found herself listening out for Bruno. One ear on the movie, one on the bedroom upstairs, and she didn't know whether she listened out of fear for the alien or yearning for the child.

That night she slept fitfully. She dreamed of Jack.

He was sitting on a fence. Behind him was a beautiful dawn. She was begging him to come home. But he remained on the fence, neither in her world nor the next. When she awoke, her pillow was soaked with tears.

Chapter 4

The following morning when Celeste went into Bruno's room, she found him sitting on his bed playing with his bear, chatting away as if to an old friend. He stopped suddenly when he saw his aunt standing in the doorway and his cheeks flushed.

'Good morning,' she said.

He held the bear against his chest. 'I'm talking to Brodie,' he explained.

'Good. Are you hungry?'

'A little,' he replied.

'Why don't you get dressed and come down and I'll make you something to eat. Do you like cereal, or toast?'

He shrugged. 'Cereal, please.'

'Your clothes are in those drawers.'

'OK.' She left the room feeling guilty that she wasn't being more helpful. Should she have taken his clothes out for him?

Bruno perked up over breakfast as Robert talked to him about football. The two of them already had a good relationship and Celeste couldn't help but feel jealous – jealous that Robert seemed to find it so easy to get over Jack's death and jealous of his ability to endear himself to his nephew. When Bruno looked at *her* his eyes darkened with apprehension. It appalled her that she could inspire such a negative reaction. She hadn't cared that she had alienated her friends and cold-shouldered her in-laws, but she cared that she caused a *child* to feel fearful. A child she was meant to be looking after. What if the shoe was on another woman's foot and the child was Jack?

After breakfast Celeste watched her husband leave, then wondered what she was going to do with Bruno all day. She was suddenly besieged by a wave of apprehension. What used she to do with Jack? Suffocating in panic, she tried to remember the things Jack had liked to do. If she couldn't think of anything today, how was she going to entertain him for *five* days?

'Can I go and play in the garden?' It was Bruno. He was standing in the doorway in his boots, his face solemn.

'Of course you can. Do you want me to come with you?' she offered, trying to inject some enthusiasm into her voice.

'I'm fine. I like exploring.'

'OK. It's a big estate. Don't get lost, now, will you?'

'I won't.'

'Why don't you take Tarquin with you?'

He smiled. 'Can I?'

'You'll be doing me a favour. That way I won't have to walk him.' Celeste put a couple of dog biscuits into Bruno's trouser pocket. 'In case he doesn't come when you call him. He's a very naughty dog, you know.'

Bruno laughed and the shadow of unease seemed to lessen slightly. 'OK,' he said.

'Marigold, will you come out of the bush!' Huxley hissed at his wife.

'I need to make sure he's OK,' Marigold replied, parting the branches to get a better look into her son's garden.

'She won't have eaten him for breakfast, you know,' said Huxley.

'Well, of course she won't. I just need to be sure that she's looking after him. You know how fragile she is.' At that moment the door opened and Bruno wandered out with Tarquin. 'Ah, there he is!'

'Alive and well?' Huxley asked.

'Very,' she replied, satisfied.

'Two arms and two legs?'

'Now you're being silly.'

'One can never be too sure.' He chuckled as he watched the dog prick his ears. 'You're going to be discovered now.'

'Damn it. Well, don't just stand there like a lemon. Help me out of this bush!'

Tarquin spotted the bush moving and trotted over, wagging his tail in anticipation of finding a large rabbit. He found Marigold instead, backing out big, round bottom first.

Bruno went after the dog, which had now

begun to bark with excitement. When he saw his grandparents, he smiled happily. 'Hello, Grandma. What are you doing here?'

'Hello, Bruno, darling. I was just looking for the football,' she replied hastily.

'Do you want to play?'

'Goodness no! I don't play. Grandpa does, though, don't you, Grandpa?'

'I don't suppose I have any choice in the matter,' Huxley replied dryly.

'Don't worry, Grandpa. I want to explore,' said Bruno.

'Do you need a guide?'

'I'm on a mission,' the child informed him importantly.

'What sort of mission? I'm good at missions.'

'To find things.'

'What sort of things?'

'Lots of things.'

'Ah, I know where to find lots of things,' said Huxley knowledgeably.

Bruno grinned. 'Then you can be my guide.'

'What a good idea. Why don't you two go off together?' Marigold suggested.

'The football is over there,' said Bruno, pointing to the bottom of the garden. 'Uncle Robert and I played yesterday.'

'Ah, so it is,' Marigold replied. 'Silly me, all that searching in the bush for nothing!'

She watched the child and his grandfather wander off through the orchard, followed by Tarquin. She turned her attention to the cottage for a moment and wondered how Celeste was. Before Jack died she would have gone in for a cup of tea and a gossip, but things had changed. Celeste avoided her most of the time. She sighed heavily and turned back towards her house. Jack had taken not only his mother's heart, but the heart out of the whole family.

Celeste stood in the hall wondering why she didn't feel relieved that Bruno had gone out to entertain himself. Instead, she felt a stab of guilt. Would he be all right on his own? What if he got lost? Was she callous to leave an eight-year-old child to his own devices? She hovered, deliberating what to do. The morning stretched out empty and quiet as before, but suddenly, now that Bruno had come to stay, the prospect of spending it alone was no longer so appealing. The house felt emptier and quieter than was comfortable.

She set about clearing away breakfast. There had only been three of them, but she took her time, putting three cups, three plates, one bowl and cutlery into the dishwasher. Then, with mounting pleasure, she climbed the stairs to tidy the child's room. He hadn't made any mess. His pyjamas were neatly folded on the bed, but he hadn't made it. This pleased her, for it gave her something to do. She stripped it bare and started again. It gave her a surprising sense of satisfaction to make it neatly, knowing that Bruno would be in it that night. She placed the slippers on the carpet and his dressing gown across the quilt. Then she stood at the window and looked out onto the summer's day. The rain had left the countryside sparkling clean and the birds were frolicking about in the sunshine. She allowed the sight to uplift her. Instead of feeling resentment she felt the first small stirrings of joy. It was as if she had looked out onto the garden but seen only her own sad reflection in the glass. Now she flung open the window and saw the vibrant green of the leaves and the sapphire blue of the sky. Fat bees buzzed about the hollyhocks and butterflies bathed their wings in the sun. She listened to the birdsong and felt the jasmine-scented breeze on her skin. For a while she forgot her pain. She surrendered to the moment and the moment was sweet.

When Bruno eventually returned, she felt a wave of relief. He hadn't got lost. His cheeks were pink and his eyes shining and he looked happy. 'Did you have fun exploring?' she asked.

'Yes, Grandpa took me up to the woods.'

'Did you see any hares? The woods are full of hares.'

'Yes, lots, and a few rabbits, too. We saw a couple of deer. They looked small, like they were baby deer.'

'They're called fawns.'

'Really? Well, we saw fawns then. They were really sweet.'

'Would you like something to drink? You must be thirsty.'

'Yes please.'

'I can make some fresh lemonade.'

'Yummy,' said Bruno.

'Come, you can make it with me, if you like.'

He shrugged. 'OK. But first I'll put my things in my bedroom.' Celeste frowned, not knowing what things he was speaking about. But she knew better than to pry into his games. She wandered into the kitchen feeling that strange stirring of joy return with more force this time.

She didn't know where her enthusiasm came from, but she didn't try to suppress it. She gave in to the desire to please and set about cutting lemons for Bruno to squeeze. He seemed to forget his earlier nervousness and warmed to the task. Together they made half a pint of juice, filled a jug with ice, water and some sugar, and gave it a good stir with a wooden spoon. 'Doesn't that look good? Just what a thirsty boy needs.'

'It looks delicious,' Bruno agreed.

'Let's see if it tastes as good as it looks.' She poured them both a glass. Bruno took a sip. He nodded and grinned over the rim. 'Good, eh?' she asked.

'Good,' he replied.

'I thought I'd cook paella for lunch. Do you like paella?'

'What's that?' he answered.

'It's a Spanish dish with prawns and rice and vegetables. It's very good. Do you want to try it?'

'Sure.'

'Good. What do you want to do now?'

'I'll go and find Grandpa,' he said and Celeste was surprised by her disappointment. She'd rather hoped he'd stay up at the cottage with her.

'OK,' she said. 'Will you come up at one for lunch? You do have a watch, don't you?' He held out his wrist for her to see the big, black watch that hung loosely on his narrow bones. 'Good.'

'Can I take Tarquin again?'

'I think he'd be very sad if you didn't take him.'

'Thank you,' he said politely, then skipped off into the sunshine.

Celeste felt her joy dissipate as the child's happy singing faded then disappeared. She thought she had entertained him making lemonade. He seemed to have enjoyed it. She certainly had. Her spirits sank into the familiar darkness and she slowly climbed the stairs. She remained a while in her bedroom, lying on her bed, her mind shutting out the twittering of birds in the garden, searching her soul for the pain as a tongue searches the mouth for the aching tooth. But before she could find it the merry chirping broke through her defences, filling her soul with delightful song. She turned onto her back and let it carry her.

A while later she found herself outside the deserted clapboard house at the bottom of the garden. The key turned easily in the lock and the door opened without a single groan of protest. She was hit suddenly by the long-forgotten smell of endeavour. She inhaled deeply and surrendered to the dizzy scents of her past. It was warm and deliciously familiar. Everything was as she had left it. Sewing machine on the long wooden table, materials piled high, boxes of buttons, sequins, lace, felt, velvet, silk and shiny baubles and tinsel. It was all tidy – she hadn't been able to work in chaos – and waiting patiently for her to take up her seat and sew again.

She struggled a moment with an unseen, though acutely recognizable, force. It was as if she had unwittingly stumbled upon herself, locked up there with the rolls of fabric, ribbon and trimmings. She hadn't even been aware that she was lost.

Then she saw Jack's quilt lying on a stool in the far corner of the room. She fought the onslaught of memories and the subdued pain burned again in her soul. She reached for it and brought the fabric to her nostrils. She closed her eyes and remembered her little boy lying sick in his bed. 'One more square to do,' she had told him. 'I wonder what I shall put on it. A bee? A tractor? What would you like, do you think?' He had smiled weakly, too ill to speak. 'Well, by the time I finish it, you will be better, my darling.' But she had never finished it.

Now tears tumbled down her cheeks, soaking into the cotton. She had never finished it because Jack had never got better. Now she never would. Then something on the floor caught her eye. She stopped crying and stared, not sure what to make of it. There, in neat rows, were cotton reels graded by colour. She caught her breath and her eyes widened.

And then she felt it. A ripple broke like a wave upon her skin and she shivered. She didn't dare move in case the feeling was lost. She closed her eyes and sensed her son.

Chapter 5

'Well, hello, young man,' said Marigold as her grandson came wandering down the garden with Tarquin. 'You've exhausted poor Grandpa,' she added, putting down the newspaper.

'Is he sleeping?' Bruno asked.

'No, he's reading in his study. Were you hoping he'd play with you?'

'I'm good,' he replied nonchalantly.

'Well, you have a friend in that silly dog.'

'He's not silly, Grandma. He's very clever.'

'Is he? I'm not entirely sure.' She smiled and patted the bench beside her. 'So, what did you do with Grandpa?'

'We went to the wood to find things.'

'And did you find what you wanted?'

'Some things.' He frowned. 'Grandma, can I borrow a peacock feather?'

Marigold raised her eyebrows in surprise. 'How do you know I have peacock feathers?' The child hesitated, then his eyes widened as he seemed to struggle to find a plausible explanation. 'Did Grandpa tell you?'

'Yes,' Bruno replied. 'I need one for my project.'

'That sounds interesting. Come with me and you can choose one.'

She took his hand and led him through the French doors into the drawing room. He looked around with curiosity, for unlike his uncle's house his grandmother's was full of fascinating things. There were piles of books and magazines everywhere. Bookcases were stuffed with old, dusty-looking tomes. Collages of paintings covered all the walls and objects were crammed onto every surface: crystal grapes, bottles of coloured sand, silver trinkets and little statues of old-fashioned ladies in long dresses. There were Persian rugs on the floors and in the hall a giant fireplace dominated the room with an alcove cut into the wall beside it, crammed full of massive logs.

'Your house is very big,' he said, pulling on his grandmother's hand as he slowed down to take everything in.

'You should explore inside as well as out,' she told him.

'I will, but I might get lost in here.'

'No, you won't, unless you climb into the wardrobe. You know what happens in the wardrobe, don't you?'

'Narnia,' he replied with a grin.

'Yes, very good,' she chuckled. 'A whole new world.'

'I love stories, Grandma.'

'So do I,' she agreed.

She led him into the dining room. In the middle of the large round table was a vase of peacock feathers. They were bright against the dark mahogany of the table. 'You see, I have lots, don't I?' She leant across and pulled the vase towards them. 'Which one do you like? They're all rather spectacular. God must have had a lot of fun creating these.'

'I don't mind,' he replied.

'All right, what about this one, then?' She plucked an especially fluffy feather and handed it to her grandson. 'So what's this project?'

'I'm collecting special things.'

'What a lovely idea. What have you got so far?'

'A feather.'

'Another feather?'

'A pheasant's feather.'

'So, are you only collecting feathers for your project?'

'No, lots of things.'

'What else do you need? I might be able to help you.'

He shrugged. 'I don't know yet.'

'Well, when you know, come and tell me and I'm sure I'll be able to help you.' She smiled down at him, her turquoise eyes full of affection. 'Now, how about a biscuit?'

'Yes, please.'

'I thought so. Let's go and see what's in the kitchen. I think we might find a whole larder full of delicious things to eat.'

*

Celeste left the quilt in the clapboard house and walked up the garden to the cottage. She didn't recall having left those cotton reels in rows like that. She would have tidied them away, for sure. But then, her state of mind at that time had been so confused and unbalanced she might well have left them without noticing.

She began to make the paella. Usually when Robert was at work she snacked for lunch. She had no one to look after but herself and she felt so low she hadn't bothered even to file her nails. Yet now she had a child in the house who needed to be fed. It gave her a sense of purpose and pulled at the redundant chord that was her maternal instinct. It was a pleasant feeling to be needed. She put on her cooking apron and made a banoffi pie for good measure.

When Bruno came back for lunch she noticed the peacock feather and knew that he had been with his grandmother. While he hurried upstairs to put it in his room, she laid the table, trying to suppress the resentment that rose like a tide in her chest because the child seemed to be happy with everyone else in the family but her.

She talked to him over lunch, making an effort to be as friendly as possible. It gave her pleasure to see him eating her paella. She asked him about Australia and whether he was excited to be moving to England. He answered in monosyllables until he tasted the banoffi pie. Then he became more loquacious, forking the pudding into his mouth in great heaps. As he tucked into a second helping he told her how his sisters didn't want to move to England because they were unhappy about leaving their friends. 'My friends come with me,' he said happily.

'That's nice,' she replied.

'I have lots of friends.'

'You're a sweet boy, Bruno. I'm sure everyone wants to be your friend.'

He grinned. 'I like English boys. They're funny.'

'You think so?'

'Yeah, they make me laugh.'

'The English have a good sense of humour because we're able to laugh at ourselves. Or so they say. I'm not sure I'm very good at laughing at myself. Not recently anyway.' She noticed he was frowning at her. 'So, what are you going to do this afternoon?'

'I'd like to play with the trains.'

She felt light-headed as the tide of resentment was swept away by the compliment. 'You want to stay up here with me? How lovely. What's your favourite tea?'

'Pizza.'

'That's easy. Pizza it is, then. What do you want on top?'

'Pepperoni,' he said.

'Then that is what you shall have.'

Bruno skipped off into the playroom to play with the trains. She heard him chatting to himself as she washed up lunch. His enthusiasm was infectious and she found herself smiling. It delighted her that he was able to amuse himself without having to rely on other children.

She telephoned Robert in the wine shop and asked him to bring home a pepperoni pizza.

'How are you doing?' He had been worrying about her all day.

'He's very sweet. He's in the playroom.'

'Are *you* OK?' He could sense her smiling down the telephone.

'I'm enjoying his company, actually. He's a lovely little boy.'

'You're incredibly good to have him, Celeste. I know how hard it is for you.'

'It's not as hard as I thought it would be.' She wanted to tell him about the strange feeling she had had in the clapboard house and the cotton reels, but she didn't want to sound desperate. She *wasn't* desperate. In fact, right now, she felt more peaceful than she had been in a long time.

'I'll see you later, then.'

'Yes, see you later.'

When Robert arrived home he was surprised to find Celeste on the playroom floor, building Lego with Bruno. He was so moved it took him a moment to find his voice. The two of them were working together, chatting in low voices, concentrating on the things they were making. The sight reminded him of Jack and he put his hand to his stomach. Celeste noticed him standing there and smiled. 'Look who's come home,' she said and Bruno raised his chocolate-brown eyes and beamed a smile as bright as a ray of sunlight.

'With a pizza. I wonder who requested pepperoni pizza?'

That evening, Celeste ran the child a bath. She filled it with bubbles and sat on the lavatory seat and talked to him while he wallowed in the warm water like a little hippo. There was something very dear about his narrow shoulders and soft white skin. Although he spoke like an older child, he still had the body of a little boy. She was surprised to hear herself ask if he would like a story before going to bed.

'Mum always reads to me,' he told her earnestly.

'What kind of stories do you like?'

'Magical ones,' he replied.

'I suppose you like Harry Potter?'

His eyes shone and he nodded vigorously. 'I love Harry Potter!' he exclaimed with zeal.

'I'll go and see what I have.'

'Did Jack like Harry Potter?'

The child's question was innocent but it caught her off guard because it was so direct and delivered without the awkwardness that always accompanied the comments of adults. Most people didn't dare mention his name at all. 'Yes, he did,' she replied.

'Did he have any wands?'

'Yes, a few. They're in his bedroom.'

'Can I see them?'

Before she could think his question over, she heard herself replying, 'Yes, after bath.' Bruno didn't want to wait a moment longer than necessary. He stood up and let Celeste wrap him in a towel. She rubbed him down, feeling his small bones beneath.

With his feet still covered in bubbles he padded into the corridor. 'Which is his bedroom?'

'This one,' she replied solemnly, pushing the door open. It squeaked quietly but put up no resistance.

'Wow!' Bruno cried. 'This is an awesome room!' His big chocolate-truffle eyes swept over the tractor wallpaper and matching curtains, the surfaces covered with all sorts of toys and the big double bed that lay empty in the middle of the room, as silent as a tomb. On top of it lay a much-loved toy rabbit. Bruno lifted it off the bed. 'What's he called?'

'Horace,' Celeste replied, her eyes stinging with the threat of tears.

'Jack really loved him, didn't he? Mum read me the story of the Velveteen Rabbit where toys come alive if they're loved. I don't think that really happens.'

'I think you're right, Bruno.'

'I suppose he was alive to Jack, though. Like Brodie, my bear. He's alive to me.'

'I think you'll find wands over here,' she said. When she reached for the basket that sat on top of the desk, she saw that her fingers were trembling.

'Wow! He has loads of wands. This one's Voldemort's, awesome!' Bruno began waving it about, holding his towel up with the other hand. He peered into the basket to see what others Jack had. 'That one's Harry's, and that one,' he said, poking it with Voldemort's, 'is Dumbledore's.'

'I'm impressed you know all the names.'

'I've seen all the films,' he told her proudly. 'Stupefy!' he exclaimed, waving the wand at an imaginary adversary. The child's towel slipped and Celeste saw the gentle curve of his back and the delicate line of his spine. Her throat constricted as she remembered Jack's tender body and the countless times she had pressed her face against his thick, velvet skin and kissed him. She knelt beside Bruno and rearranged the towel. 'Don't get cold,' she said softly.

Celeste looked through the books on the shelf. Each held a tender memory of evenings spent on the bed, reading together. She pulled out one about a dragon. 'How about this one?' she suggested, holding it up.

'That looks good,' he replied. 'I like dragons.'

'Let's go and put on your pyjamas, then.'

'Do you think there were ever dragons?'

'No,' she said, walking into the corridor.

'They might have been dinosaurs.'

'Perhaps.'

He padded along behind her. 'Stupefy,' he hissed again.

Chapter 6

When Robert went upstairs he was surprised to see Bruno sitting up in bed, looking over Celeste's shoulder at the picture book. He was engrossed in the story and Celeste was reading in the same flamboyant way she had once read to Jack. Her voice shifted up and down as she took up the different roles and every now and then, when the dragon grew angry, her deep baritone made the little boy laugh out loud. Robert paused a moment and watched, his heart aching with longing.

When she finished, she closed the book. 'So, what do you think?' she asked.

'I think the dragon got what he deserved,' Bruno replied.

'I think you're right. But he learned a valuable lesson, didn't he?'

'You don't get anywhere by being mean.'

Celeste smiled. 'You most certainly don't.' She stood up. 'You sleep well, now.' The boy snuggled beneath the duvet with his bear tucked under his chin.

A moment later Robert appeared at his bedside. 'Sweet dreams, Bruno.'

'Night, Uncle Robert,' he replied. Celeste moved away but Robert bent down and gave the child a kiss on his temple.

They left the door ajar and the light on in the corridor. 'Fancy a glass of wine?' Robert asked in a quiet voice.

'Yes, I would,' she nodded.

'Good.'

They went downstairs and into the kitchen. Robert took a couple of wine glasses down from the cupboard and looked through the rack for a suitable bottle. He felt tonight merited a special vintage.

Celeste picked up a Lego plane that Bruno had made and left on the kitchen table. She turned it around in her fingers. 'Clever, isn't he?' she said.

'He's a good lad,' Robert replied.

'Shame, I think Jack and he would have got on like a house on fire.'

Robert was surprised to hear her refer to their son in this way. The name usually caused her so much pain he had learned not to mention it.

'I think you're right.' He poured her a glass of Merlot and one for himself.

She took a sip. 'I feel foolish,' she said with a sigh.

'Why?'

'I've been unreasonable. I'm sorry.'

'You've got nothing to be sorry about.'

'I've been rude to your mother.'

'She's tough. She can take it.'

'He's just a boy,' she said with a frown.

'And you've made him feel very welcome.'

She took another sip and her eyes glistened. 'I don't know why I ever thought I couldn't.'

Suddenly, they were interrupted by a peal of laughter from Bruno's bedroom upstairs. They stared at each other in bewilderment. It sounded as if Bruno was having a one-sided conversation. 'Who's he talking to?' Robert whispered.

'He talks to his bear.'

They listened some more. 'That bear must be very chatty,' Robert laughed.

Celeste smiled. 'They're *both* very chatty.'

'Shall we leave him? He's obviously having a good time up there.'

'Yes, let him enjoy himself.' She took another sip of wine. 'I'll take out some smoked salmon.'

'Great.' He watched her as she moved about the kitchen. Her face looked less tense. He didn't dare reflect on her smile in case it disappeared again.

The following morning when Celeste and Robert awoke, they heard Bruno in Jack's bedroom next door. Celeste sat up in alarm, her heart thumping jealously in her chest. Jack's room was sacred. Why hadn't she told him? Her initial instinct was to hurry in there and drag the child out. But Robert caught her arm before she made the dash out of bed. 'Celeste, what are you going to do?'

'He can't play in there!' she hissed.

'Why? He's a little boy and it's full of little boy's toys.'

'Because it's Jack's room!' Her tone was full of accusation again.

'Do you think Jack would mind?'

'It doesn't matter. *I* mind.' She tore her arm away and climbed out of bed.

Just as she reached the door to Jack's room, she hesitated. The child was chatting away. She pushed open the door and peered inside. He was sitting cross-legged on Jack's bed with Jack's Harry Potter Studio book open in front of him. His bear was lying with Jack's rabbit. He was talking softly, turning the pages, commenting on the pictures.

'Good morning, Bruno,' she said. He looked up with a start, his face turning crimson as if he had been caught doing something wicked. 'Who are you talking to?' she asked.

'No one,' he replied quickly.

'Your bear?'

His big eyes stared back at her, the expression in them wild and fearful. 'Yes, my bear,' he replied, but he wasn't a good liar.

'Darling, you're not in trouble. You can talk to whoever you like.' He seemed to relax a little then. It obviously hadn't occurred to him not to play in Jack's room. 'Are you hungry?' He nodded. 'What would you like for breakfast? Pancakes?'

'I love pancakes,' he replied, closing the book and pulling it off the bed.

'Would you like to borrow Jack's book?'

'Yes please.'

'All right, but you must look after it. Jack's things are very precious to me.'

'I will.'

'Good. Go and put on your dressing gown and I'll make you some pancakes in the kitchen.'

Celeste returned to her bedroom. Robert was getting dressed. 'So?' he enquired. 'You didn't turf him out, did you?'

'Of course not. He was talking to his bear again.'

'Good.'

'I suppose it won't do any harm to let him play in Jack's bedroom,' Celeste conceded.

'I don't think Jack would have minded,' said Robert, straightening his tie.

'Jack would have loved a friend like Bruno to play with,' said Celeste. She looked towards the door and frowned again.

Chapter 7

Bruno disappeared into the garden straight after breakfast. Robert noticed Celeste's face as she watched him leave. She looked disappointed. She turned and caught him watching her. 'He likes your parents,' she said.

'He likes you, too,' he told her. Her expression softened. She looked vulnerable. He put his arm around her waist and kissed her cheek.

'What was that for?' she asked, a weak blush seeping through the pallor.

'Do I need a reason to kiss my wife?'

'Of course not, it's just that . . . '

'I haven't kissed you for a long time.' She lowered her eyes. 'You're doing a great job. He probably wants my father to take him to the farm.'

'Yes, it's a lovely day. Perhaps they'll be cutting. He said he wanted to go on a combine.'

'I imagine they'll start at midday when the dew dries off. Why don't you go too?'

She shrugged. 'Maybe,' she replied.

Bruno didn't come back for hours. Celeste began to bite her nails with worry. The house was very quiet. She could hear the cooing of a pigeon on the roof and the twittering of birds in the trees at the bottom of the garden. She sat on the terrace, just listening. The sun shone warmly on her face and the breeze was sugar-scented. She wondered what the child was up to all on his own, wandering the estate. There were lots of places where a boy like Bruno might find entertainment. The old stables, the duck pond, the tree house and monkey swing where Robert used to play as a boy. Jack had found endless pleasure here, too. He had found all his father's old haunts by instinct rather than design, as if the grounds had contrived to show him his father's special places. He had loved nature and had never been afraid of bees or bugs. She smiled sadly to herself as she recalled the time she had found him sitting on the lawn training bumblebees to walk up his bare arms. He had never been stung, not once. They must have sensed he was fearless. Or perhaps they sensed he was a friend.

After a while sitting with her memories, she decided to bake a cake for tea. She was sure Bruno would like one. After all, cakes had been Jack's favourite things. She put on her apron and set about assembling all the ingredients on the table: butter, flour, chocolate, eggs. Jack had loved chocolate. She pulled out a large mixing bowl and a wooden spoon. It felt good to be doing something creative. As she cracked the eggs into the bowl she contemplated how she was going to decorate it. Besides Lego, Tarquin and his bear, she wasn't really sure what Bruno liked. She had known all Jack's favourite things. Her heart gave a little tremor as she recalled the quilt she had been making him, each square embroidered with the things he loved best. She wondered what she would have done on the final square, had she finished it. She laboured beneath the sudden weight of her grief. Oh God, how she wished she had finished it.

Pulling herself together, she put the two round tins in the oven. Bruno would be back soon and it wouldn't be right for him to see her crying. She decided to decorate the cake with a picture of Tarquin with a bone. That was easy enough for a creative person like Celeste. She mixed the yellow icing for the dog and white for the bone and waited for the cake to bake. Then she wandered onto the terrace and listened out for Bruno's voice. She heard nothing but the birds and the rattling sound of a tractor in the distance.

When the cake had cooled she began to ice it. Her concentration took her out of herself and she forgot all about her pain. Her world was reduced to that small surface of cake where she carefully drew the dog with his bone, taking great care with the details, as an artist does with her paints. Her breathing grew slow, her shoulders dropped, her creativity, stifled for so long by sorrow, began to flow freely again. She felt the tentative stirring of pleasure, so subtle it was barely perceptible, like the first thawing of a lake after a long, hard winter.

When Bruno finally appeared in the kitchen with

his grandfather, Celeste had just put the finishing touches to her cake. She sat back and admired it.

'My dear girl, what an artist you are!' exclaimed Huxley, impressed.

'It's Tarquin!' exclaimed Bruno.

'It's for you,' said Celeste. 'I hope you like chocolate cake.'

'I love it!' Bruno exclaimed.

'I'm partial to a bit of chocolate cake myself. Why don't we come up for tea and help you eat it?' Huxley suggested.

'Oh, all right,' Celeste replied, surprised. 'I mean, yes, what a good idea. Of course Bruno should spend time with his grandparents.'

'Grandpa has been helping me find things,' said Bruno.

'Really? What things?' Celeste asked.

'He needs a box to put them all in,' Huxley told her. 'I said you'd have one. It's just the sort of thing Aunt Celeste would have, I said.'

'How big?' Bruno put out his hands. 'Gosh, that's quite big. What are you going to put in it?'

'Things,' said Bruno mysteriously.

'All right. Let me see.' She disappeared into the larder, returning a moment later with an old dog biscuit box. 'Will this do?'

Bruno's eyes lit up. 'Yes,' he said. She then noticed the horseshoe in his hands. Carefully he laid it inside.

'Where did you get that?' she asked.

'At the stables,' Bruno replied. 'There aren't any horses, though.'

'We sold Jack's pony,' Celeste told him. 'He didn't need it any more.'

'Right, Bruno,' said Huxley. 'Here are some more things for your box.' He dug into his pockets and pulled out a long, grey feather, a leaf half-eaten by caterpillars, and a handful of nuts taken from the sacks of bird food in Huxley's workshop.

'Gosh, you have been busy,' said Celeste. Bruno didn't reply; he was carefully placing them all at the bottom of the box so that they didn't collide with each other. 'Is this a box of special things?' she asked.

'Very special things,' Bruno replied solemnly. 'Favourite things.' He picked up the box and wandered off in the direction of the playroom.

'He's a very unusual child,' said Huxley. 'We've

spent all morning looking for those things and nothing else would do. He seemed to know exactly what he wanted. He's exhausted me. I think I'll go home and put my feet up. You can go with him tomorrow.'

She smiled, puzzled. 'I shall.'

After lunch, during which Bruno told her all about his school in Sydney, he disappeared into the playroom to build some more Lego. Celeste washed up and listened as he chatted away to himself. He seemed perfectly happy on his own. She gazed out of the window at the finches diving in and out of the bushes, and was momentarily drawn out of her thoughts. There was something about their cheerful frolicking that uplifted her own spirits.

'Aunt Celeste.' It was Bruno, standing in the doorway, a solemn look on his face.

'Oh, hi, Bruno.'

'Can we go to Grandma's house?' he asked her.

'Really, what for?'

He shrugged. 'I'd like to.'

'I suppose we could take the cake and eat it down there. Would you like that?'

'Yes,' he replied.

A few moments later they were walking through the garden with the cake carefully stored in a pretty tin. Bruno had found a little box from the playroom and was carrying it in his hand. 'What's that for?' she asked him.

He shrugged again. 'In case I find something.'

'It'll have to be a small something.'

'Yes, it will,' he agreed, skipping off ahead.

When they reached the house Marigold was on the telephone in the sitting room, her feet up on a stool, a cup of tea on the table beside her. As soon as she saw Bruno she wound up the conversation. 'Must go, Valerie. My grandson has just appeared.' She smiled broadly. 'Well, hello, darling. How are you getting on? You've exhausted Grandpa, he's gone upstairs for a little sleep.'

'We've brought you a cake,' said Bruno.

Celeste appeared behind him with the tin. 'I made it this morning.'

'I love cake,' Marigold exclaimed. 'Is it chocolate?'

The child nodded. 'And Aunt Celeste has put a picture of Tarquin on it.'

'Well, isn't she clever! Celeste, do come in and sit down.' Before she could offer Bruno a chair, he had disappeared into the hall. His footsteps could be heard running up the stairs. 'Where's he off to in such a hurry?' Marigold asked.

Celeste perched on the edge of the sofa and put the tin on her lap. She didn't look as if she was intending to stay very long. 'I don't know. He really wanted to come down here. It seems to be some kind of treasure hunt.'

'How nice!' Marigold gushed. 'Such a sweet little thing, isn't he?'

'Very,' Celeste replied.

'Huxley said that he was very clear about what he had to find this morning. He dragged poor Grandpa all over the estate.'

'I've told him I'll go with him tomorrow.'

'That's very sweet of you, Celeste.' Marigold paused and her features softened into a kind smile. 'Tell me, dear, how are *you*?'

Celeste took a deep breath and dropped her gaze to the cake tin. 'I'm sorry I was rude, Marigold. It was unforgivable.'

Marigold waved a hand in the air to dispel any hard feelings. 'Don't be silly. You've been through a really rotten time, you're entitled to be as rude as you like.'

'No, I'm not. I didn't think I'd cope with having a child in the house again. But he's just a boy, isn't he? A little boy.'

'Yes, he is.'

'I think Jack and he would have been good friends. Jack liked Harry Potter and exploring, too.'

Marigold was surprised that Celeste was speaking openly about Jack. 'It's a great shame,' she said, because she didn't know what else to say. Everything sounded like a gross understatement when it came to Jack.

'He reminds me very much of him,' Celeste continued.

'Does he?'

'Yes.' Celeste's eyes began to well with tears. 'He reminds me how little Jack was.'

At that moment, as Celeste's tears threatened to overflow, Bruno wandered into the room out of breath. 'Where have you been, darling?' Marigold asked him.

'Into the attic.'

'What on earth were you doing up there?'

'I found a dead butterfly.' He walked over and showed his grandmother the box. She took it carefully and opened it. Sure enough, there, carefully nestled in cotton wool, was a perfect Painted Lady.

'Just the thing for that box,' said Celeste.

'I know,' he replied, beaming proudly.

'You're so clever, Bruno,' Marigold exclaimed. 'So, what's next?'

'Cake,' he replied.

Marigold laughed. 'What a good idea, darling. I'll give Grandpa a shout.'

A while later, Huxley emerged and they all went into the kitchen to eat the chocolate cake. Bruno squealed with delight when Celeste opened the tin to reveal Tarquin pictured on top of the cake. 'Oh, how brilliant!' Marigold exclaimed. 'You really are very talented, Celeste.'

'I loved doing it.'

'Here's a knife. Give a slice to Grandpa. No one loves chocolate cake more than him.'

Bruno giggled. 'I do,' he said and laughed some more.

'Oh, this is awfully good,' said Huxley, biting off the end of his slice. 'How do you find it, young man?'

'Good,' Bruno agreed.

'It's better than good. I'd say it's exceedingly good!' The old man's eyes sparkled as he looked upon his grandson.

'Aunt Celeste, can I have the picture of Tarquin?'

'Of course you can,' she replied and carefully cut around it and lifted it off the cake.

'Grandma, do you have something I can put it in?'

'Don't you want to eat it?' she asked.

'I want to keep it.'

'Very well.' She pointed to one of the doors off the kitchen. 'Go into the larder and you'll find some plastic containers on the floor on the right. Help yourself.' The child hurried off.

'He's like a magpie,' said Huxley. 'If he continues like this, that box will be full at the end of five days.'

'I wonder what he's going to do with all that stuff,' said Celeste.

'Georgia did say he's in his own world,' Marigold mused.

Huxley sighed and took another bite of cake. 'It's a very exciting world. I rather wish I could join him there.'

Chapter 8

'She apologized to me, you know,' said Marigold
when Celeste had left and Bruno was lying on the
floor with one of the dogs.

'I have to hand it to you, old girl. You were quite
right,' Huxley conceded. 'I wasn't so sure it would
work, but you've proved me wrong.'

Marigold grinned. 'I think I might drive off to
Alresford for a while. She thinks I'm frightfully busy
this week.'

'And what? Drive around for a few hours?'

'I don't know.' She shrugged. 'I'm meant to be
taking bridge lessons, aren't I? I can't remember what
I said now.'

He chuckled. 'I don't think she'll notice. *She's* not
into spying.' He raised his eyebrows pointedly.

'Why don't you take Bruno harvesting? I've heard the combines chomping away up there.'

'Would you like that, young man?' he asked Bruno, putting his panama on his head.

The child sat up and smiled. 'Yes please, Grandpa. That would be awesome!'

Marigold watched them leave. It gave her a warm sense of satisfaction to see grandfather and grandson going on an expedition together. It reminded her of Robert when he was the same age, following his father around like an eager puppy. It reminded her of Jack, too. She popped a chocolate truffle into her mouth to abate her sorrow.

Huxley buckled Bruno into the passenger seat of the Land Rover then set off up the farm tracks to the fields. It was a warm afternoon. The sun was as bright as molten gold, shining radiantly onto the woods and farmland below. Huxley pointed out all the birds that crossed their path, and every time he saw a hare, he exclaimed 'Fred 'are,' with relish. After a while Bruno was copying him and shouting Fred Hare at the top of his lungs, sending the startled animals leaping into the undergrowth.

At last they saw the cloud of dust in the distance and then, as they approached, the gleaming green metal of the combine, glinting sharply in the sun. A tractor and trailer waited nearby for the combine to put out its arm to unload its grain. Huxley pulled up and climbed out of the vehicle. He lifted Bruno onto the bonnet and stood hands on hips as the combine rumbled past like a metal dinosaur. 'Wow! It's so cool!' Bruno shouted over the noise. 'Can I go on it, Grandpa?'

Huxley waved at the driver. 'When he comes around again,' he replied. The child gave a shiver of excitement.

They both watched with equal fascination. Huxley, because it was a relatively new machine and he was interested to see how quickly and efficiently it cut the wheat; Bruno because he had never seen one before, except in photographs, and it was bigger and louder than he could ever have imagined. At length it put out its arm and the tractor rattled across the stubble to ride along beside it as it unloaded its wheat.

'I'm going to drive a tractor one day,' Bruno announced, jumping off the Land Rover.

'Good, we always need enthusiastic tractor drivers,' said Huxley. 'Right, it'll come round now and you can climb up.'

When the combine reached them, Huxley took his grandson's hand and led him across the field. The beast's roar was deafening, its breath hot and furious, and the child cowered a moment against his grandfather's legs. 'You'll be all right with Peter,' Huxley shouted above the clamour. He lifted him onto the ladder and Bruno climbed up and into the cabin where Peter, a rugged, bearded farmer with kind eyes, was ready to help him in.

Bruno's excitement at being in a real combine soon superseded his fear and he grinned broadly and waved at his grandfather. Huxley waved back and smiled fondly as the small figure in the cabin disappeared up the field in a cloud of dust. As the combine huffed and puffed through the wheat, Robert's four-by-four appeared through it, approaching up the track.

He drew up beside his father's Land Rover and climbed out. 'Mother told me you were here.'

'He's having a whale of time in there.'

Robert shielded his eyes against the sun and watched. 'I bet he is.'

'Celeste came down with a cake.' Huxley nodded pensively. 'That mother of yours is a shrewd old bird.'

'I thought there must be a method to her madness.'

'Celeste just needed to see beyond herself, that's all,' said Huxley wisely.

'I think she's growing fond of Bruno,' said Robert. 'I certainly am.'

'She needs to keep herself busy. Moping about the house all day will only make her more depressed. A brood of children is what she needs.' Huxley always had a knack of saying what everyone else thought but were too polite or timid to articulate.

'You're right, of course, though I wouldn't dare broach the subject. It's a painful one.'

'Life goes on, Robert. One has to accept things and move on. Life is a harsh school of learning, but one mustn't get stuck in the ruts, but rise to the next challenge. Jack brought us all immense joy and we will never forget him. But we have to accept that he completed his task here on earth and was called home. We'll all meet again one day, but for now, we have to get on with whatever we have to do down here. Jack taught us valuable lessons, he certainly taught us all a great deal about love, but his death is also a lesson in acceptance. Celeste has to learn to let him go.'

Robert put his hands in his pockets. 'I'm not sure five days with Bruno is necessarily going to crack that one, Dad.' The combine roared past them and Bruno waved excitedly from his glass cabin. Peter waved, too, and Huxley and Robert waved back.

'I think you're underestimating the lad,' said Huxley, smiling at the boy. 'The innocent joy of a child is infectious – puts the world into perspective. You don't have to be an old codger like me to notice that.'

Eventually, the combine drew to a halt once again and Bruno descended the ladder like a monkey. Any fear he might have had initially had vanished and he now felt as powerful as if he had been riding a T. Rex. 'That was awesome, Uncle Robert!' he exclaimed, eyes sparkling. 'Thank you, Grandpa.'

Huxley ruffled his hair. 'I'm sure Peter enjoyed having some company. It can get a little lonely up there on one's own.'

'Right,' said Robert. 'Teatime, I think. Are you hungry?'

'Not really,' Bruno replied. He climbed into the back of his uncle's car.

They drove down the farm tracks towards home. The light was mellowing as the sun made its slow descent. The fields looked as if they had been baked to a soft orange hue. A pheasant ran ahead of the vehicle, not sure which way to turn, seemingly oblivious that it could fly, until it finally leapt for its life into a blackberry bush. As he wasn't hungry Robert decided to show his nephew the rest of the estate. He'd been up to the woods with his grandfather and onto the farm that first day, but he hadn't seen the lake or the family chapel where Jack had been laid to rest alongside other members of his family.

He drove through an avenue of plane trees. On the right was the lake, full of geese, moorhens and wild ducks. The water shone like pink glass in the early evening light and midges and mosquitoes hovered above its surface in clusters. Somewhere, far off, a cuckoo hooted.

The chapel was an old brick and flint church, built

in the seventeenth century by Robert's ancestors. It was tradition that every family member was buried there. Robert found it slightly unnerving to know exactly where he'd end up, although it was a comfort to know that he'd be laid to rest beside his son. 'Can we go inside?' Bruno asked.

'If you like,' Robert replied. 'Celeste and I got married here, as did your grandparents and parents.'

'Mummy and Daddy got married here?' Bruno asked.

'Yes, before they went to live in Australia.'

Bruno got out and pointed at the graveyard. 'Jack's here,' he said.

'Yes, Jack's buried here. His is the grave with all the flowers. We make sure he has flowers all the time.' It was the only plot with any flowers at all. He wondered at which point one was supposed to stop.

They wandered up the path into the chapel. It was cold and smelt of the ages. Bruno didn't spend much time inside, he was more interested in playing among the gravestones. He seemed to be making a game of leaping over the headstones. While he amused himself Robert stood beside Jack's and gazed down at the grass. It was inconceivable to imagine his child's body lying in the earth. His father had a strong belief in the Afterlife. Robert wasn't sure. Right now he wanted to believe more than anything in the world.

He felt Bruno's hand in his. He stared down at the earnest face of his nephew. 'Don't be sad, Uncle Robert,' he said.

'I miss him, Bruno,' he told him. 'He was my boy.'

Bruno looked as if he was about to say something important but thought better of it. 'I'm hungry now, Uncle Robert,' he said instead, and Robert found himself wondering what the child had been about to say and why he had chosen not to.

They arrived back at the cottage in time for supper. Robert was surprised to find Celeste had let her hair down. It fell in gentle waves over her shoulders, like it had done in the old days when Jack had lifted it like a curtain to whisper into her ear. She smiled. 'What have you been doing, Bruno?'

'I went on a combine. It was awesome!' he exclaimed.

'You must be hungry.'

'I'm thirsty,' he said, walking past her to help himself to water from the tap. He now knew where everything was and didn't feel shy about making himself at home.

'Hello, darling,' said Robert to his wife. 'You look pretty.'

'Thank you,' she replied. 'I've baked a lasagne for dinner. I hope you like lasagne,' she said to Bruno.

The child shrugged. 'Sure,' he said noncommittally.

'Do you want to call your mother?' Robert asked.

'OK,' Bruno replied. Robert gave him the telephone.

While Bruno told his mother about all the exciting things he'd been doing on the farm, Celeste and Robert chatted about their day. Celeste told him about the cake she had made and that she had taken it down to his parents' to share. He told her about the old Colonel, his most demanding customer, who had complained that the bottles he had bought were corked. Then, as they paused, they heard Bruno's voice change. It went from high and excited to low and anxious. 'I haven't, Mum. I promise ... no ... I know ... yes, and I won't ... I promise.' They caught eyes, both silently wondering what he was talking about.

They decided to play Taboo, a game in which you had to describe things without saying certain key words. Bruno was extremely good at it, as Jack had been, and soon the three of them were laughing. Robert and Celeste exchanged looks every now and then, both remembering with fondness the times they had played with their son. Robert was surprised to find that the moat of grief which his wife had allowed to cut them off from each other was gradually subsiding. Celeste was slowly becoming herself again.

That night, Celeste bathed Bruno and helped him into his pyjamas. Then she read another story which he had chosen from the shelf in Jack's bedroom. They sat on the bed, snuggled up, while Robert watched from the doorway, glass of wine in hand, a misty-eyed look on his face. Then Bruno shifted down the bed, holding his bear against his chest. He said goodnight. Celeste bent down and planted a soft kiss on his forehead. Robert kissed him on the temple and pressed the covers around his face. 'Sleep well,' he said. 'Don't let Brodie keep you awake too long, will you?'

'Brodie doesn't keep me awake,' he replied. 'Brodie likes to sleep.'

'Well, don't *you* keep Brodie awake, then. He needs his rest in order to play tomorrow.'

'OK,' said Bruno. 'Goodnight.'

It was later that night, when they went to bed, that Celeste told him about the cotton reels. 'I felt him, Robert,' she told him. 'It was as if he was in the room with me, just that I couldn't see him.'

Robert didn't want to undermine her faith. 'It's a nice thought, Celeste,' he said.

'But I don't think it *was* just a thought. He was there. I know he was.'

Robert made his own leap of faith and drew her into his arms. To his surprise, she didn't object. She lay against him with her head in the crook of his neck.

'Jack would want you to be happy,' he murmured. 'He wouldn't want either of us to be sad. He'd hate to think of us spending the rest of our lives pining for him.'

'I know. If only I could be sure that he's OK where he is, then I could . . . well, I could let him go.'

'Perhaps the cotton reels were his way of reassuring you of just that.'

'I'd like to think so,' she said.

'So would I.' He kissed her forehead and felt her relax against him. They hadn't lain like that in a very long time.

Chapter 9

The fourth day of Bruno's stay, Celeste found him playing in Jack's bedroom again. He was jumping about the place with one of Jack's wands, shouting 'Reducio!' at an invisible enemy. She remained at the door a moment, watching him. He had such exuberance. It emanated from him like a fizzy light that tickled her, too, and made her feel happy. The thought of him leaving the following day made her feel surprisingly sad. 'Good morning, Harry Potter,' she said. He spun around guiltily and she wondered why he always looked so sheepish when she interrupted his games. 'What would you like to do today, young man?'

'I don't know,' he replied. 'Stupefy!' He waved the wand at her.

She put her hands up and laughed. 'I'm sorry, I'm

just a boring old muggle. I'm not sure what any of those spells mean.'

'I can show you the book, if you like,' he suggested earnestly.

'Why don't you show me over breakfast? What does Harry Potter eat first thing in the morning?'

Bruno didn't know what the young wizard ate for breakfast, but he was very certain about what *he* wanted to eat. 'Pancakes!' he exclaimed, then, remembering his manners, he added: 'Please.'

Robert joined them in the kitchen and Celeste made him coffee. 'Would you like eggs and bacon today?' she asked.

He couldn't remember the last time she had cooked him a full English breakfast. 'If it's not too much bother,' he replied. 'I see you're making pancakes for Voldemort.'

'I'm not Voldemort!' Bruno cried, giggling. 'I'm Harry Potter!'

'Really? Are you sure you're not just a muggle pretending to be Harry Potter?' said Robert, narrowing his eyes and looking him up and down suspiciously.

Bruno giggled again. 'I'm not pretending. I *am* Harry Potter!'

They ate heartily and Bruno showed his uncle and aunt Jack's Harry Potter book, explaining the magic with enthusiasm. Robert caught his wife's eye as his nephew struggled to articulate the meaning of a horcrux. Celeste's gaze lingered on his longer than normal and in her eyes there was a tenderness he hadn't seen in a long time. He smiled and she returned it with a small curling of the lips. He felt a rush of affection for her, as if she had finally put down her drawbridge and let him cross. United at last, in an unspoken understanding that Jack didn't belong to her alone, but to him also, and that she was allowing him an equal stake in ownership, an equal stake in loss.

Robert left for work and Celeste wondered what she was going to do with Bruno. She could take him into Alresford, shopping. Perhaps he'd like to see where his uncle worked. But Bruno had his own idea. 'I'd like to paint an egg,' he said.

'An egg?' Celeste asked. 'What sort of egg?'

'An egg, like the one Uncle Robert had for breakfast.'

'Oh, a hen's egg. What a good idea. I haven't painted eggs in years. I'll have paints and varnish in my office. We could do it in there. I'll paint one too, and we can thread them through with ribbon. They're so pretty. You can make one for your mother.'

'It's for my box,' said Bruno firmly.

'Oh, all right.' Celeste was now more than a little curious about his box. It was full of the strangest things. A peacock feather, a pheasant feather, a butterfly, a horseshoe, a grey feather, the top of the cake, nuts and now an egg – and those were just the things she knew about. He'd spent most of his time on the farm, collecting things. She wondered what else he had found. She wondered why he wanted all those funny objects. They couldn't possibly be for his mother. So what was he going to do with them?

She took some eggs from the fridge and made holes in the ends to blow out the yolks. When she was left with the shells, she washed them clean, then set off with Tarquin and Bruno to her office at the bottom of the garden.

It was another sunny day. A few feathery clouds floated across the sky and a glider wheeled on the warm thermals like a silent gull. The low rumble of a tractor could be heard in Huxley and Marigold's garden as the gardener cut the grass into tidy green stripes. She wandered down the lawn with Bruno, who held his box close to his chest, as if it contained treasures he was afraid of losing. As they passed the borders she noticed how unkempt they were and wondered why she had allowed them to overgrow. She had taken pride in her garden once and it had given her pleasure to see the fruits of her labours in springtime. Now the shrubs had all grown into each other, leaving no space for anything else. It had once been a celebration of colour; now it was mostly green.

Fat bees buzzed about the few flowers that thrived and Bruno stopped to watch them. 'They're big and furry,' he said. Then he opened his eyes wide and grinned, struck with an idea. 'Can I teach one to crawl up my arm?'

Celeste was astonished. That was something Jack

had always done. She didn't know other children played with bees, too. 'You might get stung,' she warned, although Jack never had. 'Come on, let's go and paint an egg. I'd stay clear of the bees if I were you.'

She unlocked the door and Bruno went in and put his box down on the table. Celeste cleared the fabrics away so they had space. Then she opened a drawer and pulled out pots of paint and brushes. She hadn't used them in years. Once she had loved to paint, but then her business got busy and she no longer had the time. Every spare moment was filled with sewing. As they set about painting their eggs she realized just how much she had missed it.

Bruno's egg was multi-coloured. His face was serious with concentration as he painted stripes and dots with a steady hand. Celeste painted hers with flowers, gluing little sequins onto their centres so that they sparkled. She hummed contentedly as she worked. It made her feel good to be creating again. 'That's pretty,' said Bruno, as he finished his.

'So is yours,' she replied.

'It's an Easter egg,' he told her proudly.

'Oh, that's nice,' she said, wondering why he had thought of Easter in the middle of summer. 'It's lovely, Bruno. You're very creative. Now, let's put it down carefully so it doesn't smudge. It would be a shame to spoil it. Do you want to do another one?'

He nodded and picked up a second egg. 'This one will be for you,' he said. He didn't dwell on his words. It seemed very natural to him that he should want to paint his aunt an egg, but Celeste treasured his words as if they were rare and precious gems, and her eyes misted.

'Thank you, Bruno,' she said softly. 'That's very sweet.'

They spent a good hour painting eggs, then while they dried, Celeste drove Bruno into Alresford to see where his uncle worked. Robert was surprised to see them and showed his young nephew around his shop while Celeste popped into the supermarket to get supplies. Instead of buying the usual things, she wandered around looking for inspiration for more exciting dishes. She noticed a glossy cookery book on sale and popped it into her trolley. She'd cook something different for supper tonight.

When she had finished shopping and loaded the bags into the car, she returned to Robert's shop. He was busy showing Bruno how to use the till. When the old Colonel came in to complain about something else, he saw the child at the counter and forgot about his ill humour. He bought a case of claret just so the boy could do the sale. 'You'll make a good salesman one day,' said the Colonel with a chuckle.

'You should come and work here more often,' said Robert, when the old man had left. 'Colonel Thackery hasn't been in such a good mood for years!'

When Celeste suggested they return home for lunch, Robert offered to take them out for a pizza. 'It's been a while since we've eaten out,' he said. Bruno skipped about the shop excitedly. Celeste was lifted by the child's exuberance and her husband's spontaneity and she chatted all the way up the street to the pizzeria.

'Bruno will have a pizza with pepperoni,' said Robert. 'What are you going to have, darling?'

She smiled and blushed at the tender way he said 'darling'. 'I'll have a pizza Fiorentina. It'll be fun to try something new.'

When Celeste and Bruno returned home in the early afternoon, Huxley was waiting to take his grandson on the combines again. 'I'll varnish the eggs while you're out,' said Celeste, and she waved them off in Huxley's Land Rover. Then she went down to her office.

She sat at the table varnishing the eggs to the sound of a pigeon cooing on her roof. It was loud and rhythmic and made her feel nostalgic for the days before Jack had fallen ill. She remembered picnics by the fields during harvest time, his wide smile when she picked him up from school, the sound of his laughter resounding across the lawn as he practised cricket with his father. She didn't cry. Memories that had given her so much pain before now gave her pleasure, but she didn't know why.

She laid the eggs carefully on sticks, then cut ribbon to thread through them. The one Bruno had painted for her was decorated with glitter and sequins and glinted in the sunlight that streamed in through the windows. She sat for a moment wondering what to do next. Then she saw Bruno's box on the end of the table. Would he mind dreadfully if she opened it and looked inside?

She thought not. After all, he had shown her the horse shoe and the butterfly. So she pulled the box across the table and lifted the lid. She frowned at the sight of so many funny things. There was a Harry Potter wand of Jack's, the butterfly, nuts, the grey feather, the leaf, the peacock's feather, the horseshoe, the dog picture she'd made out of icing. She lifted one thing after another and looked it over.

As she allowed her mind to wander she heard herself speaking out loud in the way she used to do with Jack, when they played Taboo. *The wand belongs to a wizard, so that must be Harry Potter. The grey feather has to belong to a pigeon. The pheasant feather to a pheasant, those were easy. The dead butterfly is a butterfly and the leaf, which has been eaten by caterpillars, means caterpillar because he couldn't put a live creature in a box. The horseshoe for a pony, and nuts . . . hmm, a squirrel, I think. The peacock feather for a peacock and . . .* She looked across at the egg. *Easter egg. Could that just be an Easter egg?* At that moment she felt the blood drain from her head to her toes and she was overcome with dizziness. She stood up slowly and walked over to the quilt. She barely dared breathe because she knew what she was going to find.

Her heart began to pound as she opened the quilt. She laid it on the floor, and with the pulse throbbing frantically in her temples she looked at the pictures she had sewn into the squares. Jack's favourite things: a peacock, a pheasant, a squirrel, his pony, a caterpillar, the pigeon from the movie *Valiant*, a butterfly, Harry Potter, Tarquin, and – with her eyes filled with tears she could barely make it out – the Easter Bunny. The final square lay blank.

She clutched the quilt to her chest, looking about the room with large, frightened eyes. 'Are you here, Jack? If you're here, let me see you.' She now realized that Bruno's imaginary friend was the spirit of her son. She didn't doubt it. How else could he know to collect all these things and not an object more?

She remained on the floor, with the quilt against her heart, until Bruno found her there. He saw her tearstained face and then took in the open box on the table, and he blushed the colour of a tomato. 'You've been talking to Jack, haven't you?' she asked, and the desperation in her voice sounded more like anger.

'No ... I ... ' But Bruno wasn't a very good liar. He began to tremble. His small shoulders rose to his ears as if he wished his head could disappear inside them. Then he burst into tears.

'Bruno ... ' But before she could explain he grabbed the box and hurried from the room. Celeste scrambled to her feet. She made to run after him, but when she looked into the garden he had gone.

Chapter 10

Celeste looked everywhere for Bruno, but he was nowhere to be found. She looked in Jack's bedroom and in his own. She searched the house from top to bottom, calling Bruno's name, but he didn't answer. She scoured the garden with Tarquin, but only the pigeons knew which way he'd gone and they weren't telling.

Eventually, in despair at having caused him unhappiness, she went down to find Marigold and Huxley. She found Marigold on the terrace with a large box of biscuits and a novel. When she saw her daughter-in-law hurrying down the lawn in tears, she called her husband, who was napping in the sitting room. 'My dear girl, what's happened?'

'It's Bruno. He's run off,' Celeste explained in a thin voice.

'Run off? Why?'

'I upset him.'

'How did you upset him?'

'I didn't mean to.'

Huxley appeared through the French doors. 'What's going on?' he asked.

'Bruno's run off,' said Marigold. 'Celeste says she's upset him.'

'Well, he was a very happy chap when I dropped him off at the cottage.'

'But then he found me,' said Celeste, unable to remain still.

'Do sit down, dear,' said Marigold. 'Your fidgeting is making me dizzy. He found you, doing what?'

'I was looking through his special box.'

'And that upset him?' Marigold persisted.

'No, it upset him that I found out he'd been talking to Jack.' Huxley and Marigold were now lost for words. They glanced at each other and Celeste knew they suspected she had gone mad. 'Every object in the box corresponds with a square on the quilt I was making Jack. The peacock feather, his pony, Harry Potter, the butterfly. Each one. How could he have known if he hadn't been talking to Jack?'

'Well, I can't imagine,' said Marigold.

'And he's run off, has he?' said Huxley, impatient now to get back to the problem of Bruno's disappearance. 'I think you'd better call Robert,' he said.

'I'll call him,' volunteered Marigold, pushing herself up. 'Why don't you look around our garden, Celeste; and Huxley, you go up to the farm. He can't have gone far. He's only got little legs.'

'I'm so worried.' Celeste began to bite her nails. 'He was crying.'

Huxley patted her on the back. 'We'll find him,' he said, and his voice was so reassuring Celeste was certain that they would.

Robert arrived in a cloud of dust. He pulled up outside his parents' house and hurried round to the terrace where his mother and Celeste were now anxiously waiting. Celeste threw herself into his arms. 'I've scared him away,' she sobbed. 'Oh Robert, I've scared him away when I only meant to ask him about Jack.'

'What's going on?' he asked, confused.

Celeste pulled away and dried her eyes. She knew she had to pull herself together in order to find Bruno. She told him about Bruno's box and the quilt. 'All the time we thought he was talking to an imaginary friend, he was talking to Jack.' Robert looked sceptical. 'He sees him,' she insisted. 'No doubt about it. He sees Jack.' At that moment her father-in-law strode round the corner.

'No luck at the farm,' he said, shaking his head.

'No luck in the garden, either,' Celeste informed him. 'And I took Tarquin to sniff him out.'

'He's good at that,' said Marigold dryly.

'Now we mustn't panic,' said Robert. 'He's hurt because he clearly thought you were cross with him, Celeste.'

'Why would I be cross?'

'Because you sometimes sound cross when you're upset, darling,' he told her, not unkindly.

Celeste dropped her shoulders in defeat. 'You're right. I did sound like I was cross. I didn't mean to.

Now he's gone and it's all my fault. He doesn't realize how fond I am of him.'

Robert rubbed his chin thoughtfully. 'You say the box is full of Jack's things.'

'Yes,' Celeste answered eagerly.

'He didn't want you to have it?'

'No, he took it with him.'

'Then he's taking it to Jack.'

Celeste looked bewildered. 'But how can he?'

'The chapel. I took him there yesterday. Now I think about it, he did say a funny thing when we arrived. He said, "Jack's here." I thought he meant Jack's grave. What if he actually meant Jack, the boy?'

Celeste's fingers hovered about her lips. 'Then we must go to the chapel immediately.'

'I'm coming with you,' said Marigold, but Huxley held her back.

'No, old girl. I think they should go alone.'

Marigold was disappointed. 'Oh, all right,' she conceded, looking to her son for a hint of encouragement, but none came. She watched them walk around to the front of the house and disappear.

'This is all most irregular,' said Huxley, not sure what to make of it.

'It's wonderful,' sniffed Marigold. 'All the time we've been thinking Jack's gone, he's been with us, trying to let us know he's still present. I think I need a little fortification. Would you mind, darling?'

'You sit down and I'll go and pour us both a glass of wine. I do hope they find him. Georgia will be very cross with us if she turns up to fetch him tomorrow to find that we've mislaid him.'

The sun was now beginning to set and the birds were roosting noisily in the pine trees that circled the graveyard. As Robert switched off the car engine, they saw Bruno's small figure huddled beside Jack's grave. The child turned to see who it was, then, seeing his aunt and uncle getting out of the car, turned away sheepishly. Celeste was sure he had made himself even smaller. 'Bruno!' she cried, hurrying across the grass. 'Darling, I'm not cross. Not at all. Please don't think I am.' When she reached him he was hovering over his box, like a beggar over a sentimental treasure. He'd laid all the contents on the ground by the headstone and was now staring at them tearfully. Robert caught up with his wife. When he saw the objects so carefully displayed, he felt a lump lodge in his throat. Usually so adept with words, he now didn't know what to say.

Celeste crouched down and put her arm around the child. 'I'm not cross. In fact, I'm very happy. You've made me very happy, Bruno, and I never thought I'd ever be happy again.'

Bruno wiped his nose with the back of his hand. 'Mum told me to keep it secret,' he said.

'Your gift?'

'She says people will think I'm weird.'

'We don't think you're weird, do we, darling?'

'No, we certainly don't,' Robert croaked.

'It's nothing to be ashamed of. It's a beautiful thing to see spirits, Bruno. I only wish that I had your gift.' With her heart thumping wildly behind her ribcage, she gently probed into the boy's magical world. 'What's he like, Bruno?' she whispered. 'Is he happy?'

'He's happy all right, and really funny,' he replied, cheering up.

'What does he look like?'

'He's grown his hair a little because he says you always cut it.'

Celeste stared up at Robert in astonishment. 'He's right. I always did.' She laughed. 'I hated it when it fell into his eyes.'

'He has a T-shirt with a dragon on it.'

Now Celeste began to tremble with excitement. 'Red and grey? Is that the one?'

'Yes. And he has a pair of really cool trainers.'

'Oh, Bruno, you're right. He does.'

The child turned and looked at Celeste with the eyes of a wise old man. 'He's not dead, Aunt Celeste. People don't die and they don't get buried. It's a lie. He wants you to know that he's OK. That's all they ever want to tell us, that they're OK. Jack's not sick any more.' He grinned and his eyes were those of an eight-year-old boy again. 'I've been playing with him.'

'All the time?' Robert asked.

'Pretty much. He's been sending me out to find things for you.'

Then Robert asked the question his wife was too afraid to ask. 'Is he here now?'

Bruno stood up. He turned to face the pine tree which stood between the graveyard and the sun. 'Yes,' he said. 'Yes, he is.' Celeste and Robert followed Bruno's line of vision. Celeste's heart was so full of hope she thought it might burst. Robert's eyes were so misty he wasn't sure he'd see anything at all, physical or metaphysical. But then they both saw it. Only for a moment. A bright beam of sunlight shone through the branches and there, in the golden light, was the silhouette of a little boy. They couldn't see him clearly but they sensed he was smiling; and they felt a love stronger and deeper than anything they had yet experienced.

Celeste moved her hand and slipped it into Robert's. He closed his fingers around hers and held her tightly.

Epilogue

'Make sure you haven't forgotten anything,' Georgia shouted to Bruno as he ran back into the house to check his bedroom one last time. 'You've got Brodie, haven't you?' She smiled at Celeste. 'That would be disastrous if he were to leave his bear behind.'

'I've packed everything,' Celeste reassured her. 'If he's left anything behind Robert can drive it over. You're not so far away now.'

'I know. Isn't it lovely?' She sighed, enjoying the sun on the terrace and the lemonade her son and Celeste had made that morning. 'I'm so happy to be back in the UK. You can't imagine how much I've missed it.' She put her hand on Celeste's arm. 'You've been amazing. I can't thank you enough for having him.'

'I've loved it. He's a very special boy, you should be very proud of him. He couldn't have been more polite and well-mannered.'

'I worried it might be the wrong thing to ask you . . . ' Her voice trailed off awkwardly.

'Because of Jack?' Celeste asked. 'No, it was absolutely the right thing to do. Bruno has made me realize how empty my life is without children. Perhaps we'll be blessed with more.'

Georgia looked surprised and relieved. 'Gosh! Well, that would be nice.'

'I've put his suitcase in your car,' said Robert, appearing round the corner.

'Thank you, Robert. Ah, Mother!' Georgia exclaimed as her parents wandered up through the garden.

Huxley took off his panama and gave his daughter a big hug. 'How's the house?'

'Perfect!' she gushed. 'Just perfect.'

'Bruno's been a delight,' said Marigold. 'I'm afraid we're going to miss him dreadfully.'

'You can have him back any time,' Georgia laughed. 'But you'll have to have the girls too or they'll be jealous.'

'I'd love to have them all,' Marigold exclaimed. 'We'll all be fighting over Bruno, though.'

'You'll ruin the boy with all your clucking,' said Huxley. 'How on earth is the poor chap going to grow into a man with all you women mollycoddling him?'

'He'll make a fine man,' said Celeste with a smile. 'No doubt about that.'

Bruno ran out onto the terrace again. He put his arms around Tarquin and pressed his face into his fur. Then he said goodbye to his grandparents and uncle.

'You'll come back soon, I hope,' said Robert. 'I could do with your help in the shop.'

Bruno laughed. 'Yes please,' he said.

'And I have something special for you,' said Celeste, lifting a large shopping bag off the floor.

'Wow! What is it?' he asked.

'It's the quilt. I finished it last night and I would like you to have it.'

'Thank you, Aunt Celeste.'

'It's a pleasure,' she said, and winked at him.

They waved the car off until it had disappeared down the track and all that remained was settling dust. 'I'm going to start working again,' said Celeste to Robert as they walked back into the garden.

'I think that's a very good idea,' he replied, pleased.

'Me too. I really enjoyed sewing the last square. I'd forgotten how much pleasure sewing gave me.'

'So, what did you embroider on it?'

She smiled. 'The sun,' she replied.

He smiled back. 'The sun. I think that's very appropriate.'

'So do I. For more than one reason. The sun is happy. The sun is light.' She slipped her hand into his. 'Light is eternal and so is Jack.'

Read on for an excerpt from

Songs of Love and War

the new novel from Santa Montefiore

Is mise Peig Ni Laoghaire. A Tiarna Deverill, dhein tú éagóir orm agus ar mo shliocht trín ár dtalamh a thógáil agus ár spiorad a bhriseadh. Go dtí go gceartaíonn tú na h-éagóracha siúd, cuirim malacht ort féin agus d-oidhrí, I dtreo is go mbí sibh gan suaimhneas síoraí I ndomhan na n-anmharbh.

I am Maggie O'Leary. Lord Deverill, you have wronged me and my descendants by taking our land and breaking our spirits. Until you right those wrongs I curse you and your heirs to an eternity of unrest and to the world of the undead.

Maggie O'Leary, 1662

Prologue

The two little boys with grubby faces and scuffed knees reached the rusted iron gate by way of a barely distinguishable track that branched off the main road and cut through the forest in a sleepy curve. On the other side of the gate, forgotten behind trees, were the charred remains of Castle Deverill, once home to one of the grandest Anglo-Irish families in the land before it was consumed in a fire three years before. The drystone wall that encircled the property had collapsed in places due to neglect, the voracious appetite of the forest and harsh winter winds. Moss spread undeterred, weeds seeded themselves indiscriminately, grass grew like tufts of hair along the top of the wall and ivy spread its leafy fingers over the stones, swallowing entire sections completely so that little of it remained to be seen. The boys were unfazed by the large sign that warned trespassers of prosecution or the dark driveway ahead that was littered with mouldy leaves, twigs and mud, swept onto it season after desolate season. The padlock clanked ineffectively against its chain as the boys pushed the gates apart and slipped through.

On the other side, the forest was silent and soggy, for the summer was ended and autumn had blown in with icy gales and cold rain. Once, the drive had been lined on either side with red-rhododendron bushes but now they were partly obscured by dense nettles, ferns and overgrown laurel. The boys ran past them, oblivious of what the shrubs represented, unaware that that very drive had once witnessed carriages bearing the finest in the county to the magnificent castle overlooking the sea. Now the drive was little more than a dirt track and the castle lay in ruins. Only ravens and pigeons ventured there, and intrepid little boys intent on adventure, confident that no one would discover them in this forgotten place.

The children hurried excitedly through the wild grasses to play among the remnants of the once stately rooms. The sweeping staircase had long gone and the centre chimneys had fallen through the roof and formed a mountain of bricks below for the boys to scale. In the west wing the surviving part of the roof remained as sturdy beams that straddled two of the enduring walls, like the exposed ribcage of a giant animal left to decay in the open air.

The boys were too distracted to feel the sorrow that hung over the place or to hear the plaintive echo of the past. They were too young to have an awareness of nostalgia and the melancholic sense of mortality it induces. The ghosts who dwelt there, mourning the loss of their home and their brief lives, were as wind blowing in off the water. The boys heard the moaning of the empty windows and the whistling about the remaining chimney stacks and felt only a frisson of exhilaration, for the eeriness served to enhance their pleasure, not diminish it. The ghosts might as well have been alone for the attention the boys paid them.

Over the front door, one of the boys was able to make out some Latin letters, tarnished by soot, half-concealed in the blackened lintel. '*Castellum Deverilli est suum regnum 1662,*' he read out.

'What does that mean?' asked the smaller boy.

'Everyone around here knows what that means. A Deverill's castle is his kingdom.'

The smaller child laughed. 'Not much of a kingdom now,' he said.

They went from room to room in the fading light like a pair of urchins, excavating hopefully where the ground was soft. Their gentle chatter mingled with the croaking of ravens and the cooing of pigeons, and the ghosts were appeased as they remembered their own boyhoods and the games they had played in the sumptuous gardens of the castle. For once, the castle had been magnificent.

At the turn of the century there had been a walled garden, abundant with every sort of fruit and vegetable to feed the Deverill family and their servants. There had been a rose garden, an arboretum and a maze where the

117

Deverill children had routinely lost themselves and each other among the yew hedges. There had been elaborate glass houses where tomatoes had grown among orchids and figs, and yellow cowslips had reflected the summer sun in the wild-flower garden where the ladies of the house had enjoyed picnics and afternoons full of laughter and gossip. Those gardens had once been a paradise but now they smelt of decay. A shadow lingered in spite of the sunshine and year after year bindweed slowly choked the gardens to death. Nothing remained of the castle's former beauty, except a savage splendour of sorts, made all the more arresting by its tragedy.

At the rattling sound of a motor car the boys stopped their digging. The noise grew louder as the car advanced up the drive. They looked at each other in bewilderment and crept hastily through the rooms to the front, where they peered out of a glassless window to see a shiny Ford Model T making its way past the castle before halting at the steps leading up to where the front door had once been.

Consumed with curiosity, they elbowed each other in their effort to get a closer look, while at the same time careful to keep their heads concealed behind the wall. The boys' jaws fell open at the sight of the car with its soft top and smoothly curved lines. The sun bounced off the sleek green bonnet and the silver headlights shone like frog's eyes. Then the driver's door opened and a man stepped out wearing a brown felt hat and smart camel coat. He swept his eyes over the castle, taking a moment to absorb the dramatic vision. He shook his head and pulled a face as if to acknowledge the sheer scale of the misfortune that had destroyed such a beautiful castle. Then he walked round to the passenger door and opened it.

He held out his hand and a small black glove reached out and took it. The boys were so still that, were it not for their pink faces and black hair, they might have been a pair of mischievous cherub statues. With mounting interest they watched the woman step out. She wore an elegant dress of a deep emerald green and a long black coat, with a black cloche hat pulled low over her face. Only her scarlet lips could be seen below it, somehow shocking against her white skin. Glittering beneath her right shoulder was a large diamond star brooch. The boys' eyes widened for she looked as if she came from another world; the sort of world that had once inhabited this fine castle before it was swept away.

The woman stood at the foot of the darkened walls and lifted her chin. She took the man's hand and turned to face him. 'As God is my witness,' she said, and the boys had to strain their ears to hear her. 'I will rebuild this castle.' She paused and the man made no move to hurry her. At length she returned her gaze to the castle and her jaw stiffened. 'After all, I have as much right as any of the others.'

PART ONE

Chapter 1

Kitty Deverill was nine years old. For other children, born on other days, turning nine was of no great significance. But for Kitty, born on the ninth day of the ninth month in the year 1900, turning nine had been very significant indeed. It wasn't her mother, the beautiful and narcissistic Maud, who had put those ideas into the young child's head; Maud was not interested in Kitty. She had two other daughters who were soon to come of age and a cherished son at Eton who was the light in his mother's eyes. In the five years between Harry and Kitty's births Maud had suffered three miscarriages induced by riding hard over the hills around Ballinakelly; Maud did not want her pleasure halted by an inconvenient pregnancy. However, no amount of reckless galloping managed to unburden her of her fourth child, who, contrary to expectation, was a weak and squeaking girl with red hair and transparent skin, more like a scrawny kitten than a human baby. Maud had turned her face away in disgust and refused to acknowledge her. In fact, she had quite rejected her child, declining to allow her friends to visit, donning her riding habit and setting off with the hunt as if the birth had never happened. For a woman so enraptured with her own beauty an ugly baby was an affront. No, Maud would never have put ideas into Kitty's head that she was in any way special or important.

It was her paternal grandmother, Adeline, Lady Deverill, who told her that the year 1900 was auspicious and that her date of birth was also remarkable, on account of it containing so many nines. Kitty was a child of Mars, Adeline would remind her when they sat together in Adeline's private sitting room on the first floor, one of the few rooms of the castle that was always warm. This meant that her life would be defined by conflict – a testing hand of cards dealt by a God who surely knew that Kitty would rise to the challenge with courage and wisdom. Adeline told her much else, besides, and Kitty far preferred her stories of angels and demons to the dry tales her Scottish governess read her, and even to the kitchen maids' tittle-tattle, mostly local gossip Kitty was too young to understand. Adeline Deverill knew about *things*. Things at which Kitty's grandfather rolled his eyes and dismissed as 'blarney', things her father mocked with affection and things that caused Kitty's mother great concern. Maud Deverill was less amused by tales of spirits, stone circles and curses and instructed Miss Grieve, Kitty's Scottish governess, to punish the child if she ever indulged in what she considered to be 'ghastly peasant superstition'. Miss Grieve, with her tight lips and tight vowels, was only too happy to whack the palms of Kitty's hands with a riding crop. Therefore the child had learned to be secretive. She had grown as furtive as a fox, indulging her interest only with her grandmother, in the warmth of her little den that smelt of turf fire and lilac.

Kitty didn't live in the castle: that was where her grandparents lived and what, one day, her father would inherit, along with the title of Lord Deverill, dating back to the seventeenth century. Kitty lived on the estate in the old Hunting Lodge, positioned by the river, within walking distance of the castle. Overlooked by her mother and too cunning for her governess, the child was able to run wild about the gardens and surrounding countryside and to play with the local Catholic children who took to the fields with their Tommy cans. Had her mother known she would have developed a fever and retired to her room for a week to get over the trauma. As it was, Maud was often so distracted that she seemed to forget entirely that she had a fourth child and was irritated when Miss Grieve reminded her.

Kitty's greatest friend and ally was Bridie, the raven-haired daughter of Lady Deverill's cook, Mrs Doyle. Born in the same year, only a month apart, Kitty believed them to be 'spiritual sisters' due to the proximity of their birth dates and the fact that they had been thrown together at Castle Deverill, where Bridie would help her mother in the kitchen, peeling potatoes and washing up, while Kitty loitered around the big wooden table stealing the odd carrot when Mrs Doyle wasn't looking. They might have different parents, Kitty told Bridie, but their souls were eternally connected. Beneath their material bodies they were creatures of light and there was very little difference between them. Grateful for Kitty's friendship, Bridie believed her.

Because of her unconventional view of the world, Adeline was happy to turn a blind eye to the girls playing together. She loved her strange little granddaughter who was so much like herself. In Kitty she found an ally in a family who scoffed at the idea of fairies and trembled at the mention of ghosts while claiming not to believe in them. She was certain that souls inhabited physical bodies in order to live on earth and learn important lessons for their spiritual evolution. Thus, a person's position and wealth was merely a costume required for the part they were playing and not a reflection of their worth as a soul. In Adeline's opinion a tramp was as valuable as a king and so she treated everyone with equal respect. What was the harm of Kitty and Bridie enjoying each other's company? she asked herself. Kitty's sisters were too old to play with her, and Celia, her English cousin, only came to visit in the summer, so the poor child was friendless and lonely. Were it not for Bridie, Kitty might be in danger of running off with the leprechauns and goblins and be lost to them forever.

One story in particular fascinated Kitty above all others:

the Cursing of Barton Deverill. The whole family knew it, but no one besides Kitty's grandmother, and Kitty herself, believed it. They didn't just believe, they *knew* it to be true. It was that knowing that bonded grandmother and granddaughter firmly and irreversibly, because Adeline had a gift she had never shared with anyone, not even her husband, and little Kitty had inherited it.

'Let me tell you about the Cursing of Barton Deverill,' said Kitty to Bridie one Saturday afternoon in winter, holding the candle steady in their dark lair beneath the back staircase, which was an old, disused cupboard in the servants' quarters of the castle. The light illuminated Kitty's white face so that her big grey eyes looked strangely old, like a witch's, and Bridie felt a shiver ripple across her skin, something close to fear. She had heard her mother speak of the Banshee and its shriek that pre-warned of death.

'Who was Barton Deverill?' Bridie asked, her musical Irish accent in sharp contrast to Kitty's clipped English vowels.

'He was the first Lord Deverill and he built this castle,' Kitty replied, keeping her voice low for dramatic effect. 'He was a right brute.'

'What did he do?'

'He took land that wasn't his and built on it.'

'Who did the land belong to?'

'The O'Learys.'

'The O'Learys?' Bridie's black eyes widened and her cheeks flushed. 'You don't mean *our* Jack O'Leary?'

127

'The very same. I can tell you there is no love lost between the Deverills and the O'Learys.'

'What happened?'

'Barton Deverill, my ancestor, was a supporter of King Charles I of England. When his armies were defeated by Cromwell, he ran off to France with the King. Later, when King Charles II was crowned, he rewarded Barton for his loyalty with a title and these lands where he built this castle. Hence the family motto: A Deverill's castle is his kingdom. The trouble was those lands didn't belong to the King, they belonged to the O'Learys. So, when they were made to leave, old Maggie O'Leary, who was a witch . . . '

Bridie laughed nervously. 'She wasn't really a witch!'

Kitty was very serious. 'She was so. She had a cauldron and a black cat that could turn a person to stone with one look of its big green eyes.'

'Just because she had a cauldron and a cat doesn't mean she was a witch,' Bridie argued.

'Maggie O'Leary was a witch and everyone knew it. She put a curse on Barton Deverill.'

Bridie's laughter caught in her throat. 'What was the curse?'

'That Barton Deverill and every male heir after him will never leave Castle Deverill but remain between worlds until an O'Leary returns to live on the land. It's very unfair because Grandpa and Father will have to hang around here as ghosts, possibly forever. Grandma says that it is very unlikely that a Deverill will ever marry an O'Leary!'

'You never know. They've come up in the world since then,' Bridie added helpfully, thinking of Jack O'Leary whose father was the local vet.

'No, they are all doomed, even my brother Harry.' Kitty sighed. 'None of them believes it, but I do. It makes me sad to know their fate.'

'So, are you telling me that Barton Deverill is still here?' Bridie asked.

Kitty's eyes widened. 'He's still here and he's not very happy about it.'

'You don't really believe that, do you?'

'I *know* it,' said Kitty emphatically. 'I can *see* him.' She bit her lip, aware that she might have given too much away.

Now Bridie was more interested. She knew her friend wasn't a liar. 'How can you see him if he's a ghost?'

Kitty leaned forward and whispered, 'Because I see dead people.' The candle flame flickered eerily as if to corroborate her claim and Bridie shivered.

'You can see dead people?'

'I can and I do. All the time.'

'You've never told me before.'

'That's because I didn't know if I could trust you.'

'What are they like, dead people?'

'Transparent. Some are light, some are dark. Some are loving and some aren't.' Kitty shrugged. 'Barton Deverill is quite dark. I don't think he was a very nice man when he was alive.'

'Doesn't it scare you?'

'It used to, until Grandma taught me not to be afraid. She sees them too. It's a gift, she says. But I'm not allowed to tell anyone.' She unconsciously rubbed the palm of her hand with her thumb.

'They'll lock you away,' Bridie said and her voice quivered. 'They do that, don't you know. They lock people away in the red-brick in Cork City for less and they never come out. Never.'

'Then you'd better not tell on me.'

'Oh, I wouldn't.'

Kitty brightened. 'Do you want to see one?'

'A ghost?'

'Barton Deverill.'

The blood drained from Bridie's cheeks. 'I don't know . . .'

'Come on, I'll introduce you.' Kitty blew out the candle and pushed open the door.

The two girls hurried along the passageway. Regardless of the disparity of their colouring, they could have been sisters as they skipped off together for they were similar in height and build. However, there was a marked difference in their clothes and countenance. While Kitty's dress was white, embellished with fine lace and silk, tied at the waist with a pale blue bow, Bridie's was brown and shapeless and made from a coarse, scratchy frieze. Kitty wore black lace-up boots that reached mid-calf, and thick black stockings, while Bridie's feet were bare and dirty. Kitty's governess brushed her hair and pinned it off her face with ribbons; Bridie received no such attention and her hair was tangled and unwashed, almost reaching as far as her waist. The difference was not only marked in their attire but in the way they looked out onto the world. Kitty had the steady, lofty gaze of a child born to privilege and entitlement, while Bridie had the feral stare of a waif who was always hungry, and yet there was an underlying need in Kitty that bridged the gap between them. Were it not for the loving company of her grandparents and the sporadic attention lavished on her by her father when he wasn't out hunting, shooting game or at the races, Kitty would have been starved of love. It was this longing that gave balance to their friendship, for Kitty needed Bridie just as much as Bridie needed her.

While Kitty was unaware of these differences, Bridie, who heard her parents and brothers complaining endlessly about their lot, was very conscious of them. However, she liked Kitty too much to give way to jealousy, and she was too flattered by her friendship to risk losing it. She accepted her position with the passive compliance of a sheep.

The two girls heard Mrs Doyle grumbling to one of the maids in the kitchen but they scurried on up the back staircase as quiet as kittens, aware that if they were caught their playtime would be over and Bridie summoned to wash up at the sink.

No one ever went up to the western tower. It was chilly and damp at the top of the castle and the spiral staircase was in need of repair. Two of the wooden steps had collapsed and

Kitty and Bridie had to jump over the gaps. Bridie breathed easily now because no one would find them there. Kitty pushed open the heavy door at the top of the stairs and peered around it. Then she turned back to her friend. 'Come,' she whispered. 'Don't be frightened. He won't hurt you.'

Bridie's heart began to race. Was she really going to see a ghost? Kitty seemed so sure. Tentatively and with high expectations, Bridie followed Kitty into the room. She looked at Kitty. Kitty was smiling at a tatty old armchair as if someone was sitting in it. But Bridie saw nothing besides the faded burgundy silk. However, the room was colder than the rest of the castle and she shivered and hugged herself in a bid

to keep warm.

'Well, can't you see him?' Kitty asked.

'I can't see anything,' said Bridie, wanting to very much.

'But he's *there*!' Kitty exclaimed, pointing to the chair. 'Look *harder*.'

Bridie looked as hard as she could until her eyes watered. 'I don't doubt you, Kitty, but I can see nothing but the chair.'

Kitty was visibly disappointed. She stared at the man scowling in the armchair, his feet propped up on a stool, his hands folded over his big belly, and wondered how it was possible for her to see someone so clearly when Bridie couldn't. 'But he's right in front of your nose. This is my friend, Bridie,' Kitty said to Barton Deverill. 'She can't see you.'

Barton shook his head and rolled his eyes. That didn't surprise him. He'd been stuck in this tower for over two hundred years and in all that time only the very few had seen him – most unintentionally. At first it had been quite amusing being a ghost but now he was bored of observing the many generations of Deverills who came and went, and even more disenchanted by the ones, like him, who remained stuck in the castle as spirits. He wasn't keen on company and there were now too many furious Lord Deverills floating about the corridors to be easily avoided. This tower was the only place he could be free of them, and their wrath at discovering suddenly, upon dying, that the Cursing of Barton Deverill was not simply a family legend but an immutable truth. With the benefit of hindsight, they would have gladly taken an O'Leary for a bride and subsequently ensured their eternal rest as a free soul in Paradise. As it was they were too late. They were stuck and there was nothing they could do about it except rant at *him* for having built the castle on O'Leary land in the first place.

Now Barton turned his jaded eyes onto the eerie little girl whose face had turned red with indignation, as if it were somehow *his* fault that her plain friend was unable to see him. He folded his arms and sighed. He wasn't in the mood for conversation. The fact that she sought him out from time to time did not make her his friend and did not give her permission to show him off like an exotic animal in a menagerie.

Kitty watched him stand up and walk through the wall. 'He's gone,' she said, dropping her shoulders in defeat.

'Where?'

'I don't know. He's quite bad-tempered, but so would *I* be if I were stuck between worlds.'

'Shall we leave now?' Bridie's teeth were chattering.

Kitty sighed. 'I suppose we must.' They made their way back down the spiral staircase. 'You won't tell anyone, will you?'

'I cross my heart and hope to die,' Bridie replied solemnly, wondering suddenly whether her friend wasn't a little over-imaginative.

In the bowels of the castle Mrs Doyle was expertly making butterballs between two ridged wooden paddles, while the scrawny kitchen maids were busy peeling potatoes, beating eggs and plucking fowl for that evening's dinner party, to which Lady Deverill had invited her two spinster sisters, Laurel and Hazel, known affectionately as the Shrubs, Kitty's parents, Bertie and Maud, and the Rector and his wife. Once a month Lady Deverill invited the Rector for dinner, which was an obligation and a great trial because he was greedy and pompous and prone to spouting unsolicited sermons from his seat at her table. Lady Deverill didn't think much of him, but it was her duty as Doyenne of Ballinakelly and a member of the Church of Ireland, so she instructed the cook, brought in flowers from the greenhouses and somewhat mischievously invited her sisters to divert him with their tedious and incessant chatter.

When Mrs Doyle saw Bridie she pursed her lips. 'Bridie, what are you doing loitering in the corridor when I have a banquet to cook? Come and make yourself useful and pluck this partridge.' She held up the bird by its neck. Bridie pulled a face at Kitty and went to join the kitchen maids at the long oak table in the middle of the room. Mrs Doyle glanced at Kitty, who was standing in the doorway with her long white face and secretive mouth that always curled at the corners, as if she had exclusive knowledge of something important, and wondered what she was thinking. There was something in that child's eyes that put the heart crossways in her. She couldn't explain what it was and she didn't resent the girls playing together, but Bridie's mother didn't think any good would come of their friendship when, as they grew older, their lives would inevitably take them down different paths and Bridie would be left feeling the coldness and anguish of Kitty's rejection. She went back to her butter. When she looked up again Kitty had gone.

Chapter 2

Kitty's attention had been diverted by the loud crack of gunfire. She remained for a moment frozen on the back stairs. It sounded like it had come from inside the castle. There followed an eruption of barking. Kitty hurried into the hall to see her grandfather's three brown wolfhounds bursting out of the library and heading off up the staircase at a gallop. Without hesitation she ran after them, jumping two steps at a time to reach the landing. The dogs raced down the corridor, skidding on the carpet as they charged round the corner, narrowly missing the wall.

Kitty found her grandfather in his habitual faded tweed breeches and jacket at the window of his dressing room, pointing a rifle into the garden. He gleefully fired another shot. It was lost in the damp winter mist that was gathering over the lawn. 'Bloody papists!' he bellowed. 'That'll teach you to trespass on my land. Now make off with you before I aim properly and send you to an early grave!'

Kitty watched him in horror. The sight of Hubert

Deverill shooting at Catholics was not a surprise. He often clashed with the poachers and knackers creeping about his land in search of game and she had eavesdropped enough at the library door to know exactly what he thought of *them*. She didn't understand how her grandfather could loathe people simply for being Catholic – all Kitty's friends were Irish Catholics. Hubert's dogs panted at his heels as he brought the gun inside and patted them fondly. When he saw his granddaughter standing in the doorway, like a miniature version of his wife with her eyebrows knitted in disapproval, he grinned mischievously. 'Hello, Kitty my dear. Fancy some cake?'

'Porter cake?'

'Laced with brandy. It'll do you good. Put some colour in those pale cheeks of yours.' He pressed the bell for his valet, which in turn rang a little bell on a board down in the servants' quarters above the name 'Lord Deverill'.

'I was born pale, Grandpa,' Kitty replied, watching him open his gun and fold it over his arm like her grandmother held her handbag when they went into Ballinakelly.

'How's the Battle of the Boyne?' he asked.

She sighed. 'That was last year, Grandpa. I'm learning about the Great Fire of London now.'

'Good good,' he muttered, his mind now on other things.

'Grandpa?'

'Yes.'

'Do you love this castle?'

'Minus point for a silly question,' Hubert replied gruffly.

'I mean, would you mind if you were stuck here for all eternity?'

'If you're referring to the Cursing of Barton Deverill, your governess should be teaching you proper history, not folklore.'

'Miss Grieve doesn't teach me folklore, Grandma does.'

'Yes, well . . . ' he mumbled. 'Poppycock.'

'But you would be happy here, wouldn't you? Grandma says you love the castle more than any Deverill ever has.'

'You know your grandmother is always right.'

'I wonder whether you'd mind terribly living on—'

He stopped her before she could continue. 'Where the devil is Skiddy? Let's go and have some cake before the mice eat it, shall we? Skiddy!'

As they made their way down the cold corridor to the staircase they were met by a wheezing Mr Skiddy. At sixty-eight, Frank Skiddy had worked at Castle Deverill for over fifty years, originally in the employ of the previous Lord Deverill. He was very thin and frail on account of an allergy to wheat and lungs scarred by a chest infection suffered in early childhood, but the idea of retirement was anathema to the old guard who worked on in spite of their failing bodies. 'My lord,' he said when he saw Lord Deverill striding towards him over the rug, followed by his granddaughter and a trio of dogs.

'You're slowing down, Skiddy.' Hubert handed the valet his gun. 'Needs a good clean. Too many rabbits in the gardens.'

'Yes, my lord,' Mr Skiddy replied, accustomed to his master's eccentric behaviour and unmoved by it.

Lord Deverill strode on down the front stairs. 'Fancy a game of chess with your cake, young lady?'

'Yes please,' Kitty replied happily. 'I'll set up the board and we can play after tea.'

'Trouble is you spend too much time in your imagination. Dangerous place to be, one's imagination. Your governess should be keeping you busy.'

'I don't like Miss Grieve,' said Kitty.

'Governesses aren't there to be liked,' her grandfather told her sternly, as if liking one's governess was as odd an idea as liking a Catholic. 'They're to be tolerated.'

'When will I be rid of her, Grandpa?'

'When you find yourself a decent husband. You'll have to tolerate him, too!'

Kitty loved her grandparents more than she loved her parents or her siblings because in their company she felt valued. Unlike her mama and papa, they gave her their time and attention. When Hubert wasn't hunting, fishing, picking off snipe around the estate with his dogs or in Dublin at the Kildare Street Club or attending meetings at the Royal Dublin Society, he taught her chess, bridge and whist with surprising patience for a man generally intolerant of children. Adeline let her help in the gardens. Although they had plenty of gardeners, Adeline would toil away for hours in the greenhouses, with their pretty blancmange-shaped roofs. In the warm, earthy air of those glass buildings she grew carnations, grapes and peaches, and nurtured a wide variety of potted plants with long Latin names. She grew herbs and flowers for medicinal purposes, taking the trouble to pass on her knowledge to her little granddaughter. Juniper for rheumatoid arthritis, aniseed for coughs and indigestion, parsley for bloating, red clover for sores and hawthorn for the heart. Her two favourites were cannabis for tension and milk thistle for the liver.

When Hubert and Kitty reached the library, Adeline looked up from the picture of the orchid she was painting at the table in front of the bay window, taking advantage of the fading light. 'I suppose that was you, dear, at your dressing-room window,' she said, giving her husband a reproachful look over her spectacles.

'Damn rabbits,' Hubert replied, sinking into the armchair beside the turf fire that was burning cheerfully in the grate, and disappearing behind the *Irish Times*.

Adeline shook her head indulgently and resumed her painting. 'If you go on so, Hubert, you'll just make them all the more furious,' said Adeline.

'They're not furious,' Hubert answered.

'Of course they are. They've been furious for hundreds of years ...'

'What? Rabbits?'

Adeline suspended her brush and sighed. 'You're impossible, Hubert!'

Kitty perched on the sofa and stared hungrily at the cake that had been placed with the teapot and china cups on the table in front of her. The dogs settled down before the fire with heavy sighs. There'd be no cake for them.

'Go on, my dear, help yourself,' said Adeline to her granddaughter. 'Don't they feed you over there?' she asked, frowning at the child's skinny arms and tiny waist.

'Mrs Doyle is a better cook,' said Kitty, picturing Miss Gibbons's fatty meat and soggy cabbage.

'That's because I've taught her that food not only has to fill one's belly, but has to taste good at the same time. You'd be surprised how many people eat for satisfaction and not for pleasure. I'll tell your mama to send your cook up for some training. I'm sure Mrs Doyle would be delighted.'

Kitty helped herself to a slice of cake and tried to think of Mrs Doyle being delighted by anything; a sourer woman was hard to find. A moment later the light was gone and Adeline joined her granddaughter on the sofa. O'Flynn, the doddering old butler, poured her a cup of tea with an unsteady hand and a young maid silently padded around the room lighting the oil lamps. Soon the library glowed with a soft, golden radiance. 'I understand that Victoria will be leaving us soon to stay with Cousin Beatrice in London,' said Adeline.

'I don't want to go to London when I come of age,' said Kitty.

'Oh, you will when you're eighteen. You'll be weary of all the hunt balls and the Irish boys. You'll want excitement and new faces. London is thrilling and you like Cousin Beatrice, don't you?'

'Yes, she's perfectly nice and Celia is funny, but I love being here with *you* best of all.'

Her grandmother's face softened into a tender smile. 'You know it's all very well playing with Bridie here at the castle, but it's important to have friends of your own sort. Celia is your age exactly and your cousin, so it is natural that you should both come out together.'

'Surely, there's a Season in Dublin?'

'Of course there is, but you're Anglo-Irish, my dear.'

'No, I'm Irish, Grandma. I don't care for England at all.'

'You will when you get to know it.'

'I doubt it's as lovely as Ireland.'

'Nowhere is as lovely as here, but it comes very close.'

'*I* wouldn't mind if I were cursed to remain here for all eternity.'

Adeline lowered her voice. 'Oh, I think you would. Between worlds is not a nice place to be, Kitty. It's very lonely.'

'I'm used to being on my own. I'd be very happy to be stuck in the castle forever, even if I had to pass my time with grumpy old Barton. I shouldn't mind at all.'

After playing chess with her grandfather Kitty walked home in the dark. The air smelt of turf smoke and winter and a barn owl screeched through the gathering mist. There was a bright sickle moon to light her way and she skipped happily through the gardens she knew so well, along a well-trodden path.

When she reached the Hunting Lodge she crept in

through the kitchen where Miss Gibbons was sweating over a tasteless stew. Kitty could hear the sound of the piano coming from the drawing room and recognized the hesitant rendition as sixteen-year-old Elspeth's, and smiled at the thought of her mother, on the sofa with a cup of tea in her thin white hand, subjecting some poor unfortunate guest to this excruciating performance. Kitty tiptoed into the hall and hid behind a large fern. The playing suddenly stopped without any sensitivity of tempo. There was a flurry of light clapping, then she heard her mother's voice enthusiastically praising Elspeth, followed by the equally enthusiastic voice of her mother's closest friend, Lady Rowan-Hampton, who was also Elspeth's godmother. Kitty felt a momentary stab of longing. Lady Rowan-Hampton, whom her parents called Grace, was the most beautiful woman she had ever seen and the only grown-up, besides her grandparents, who made her feel special. Knowing she wasn't allowed downstairs unless summoned by her parents, Kitty reluctantly retreated upstairs by way of the servants' staircase.

The Hunting Lodge was not as large and imposing as the castle, but it was suitably palatial for the eldest son of Lord Deverill, and much larger than its modest name suggested. It was a rambling grey-stone house partly covered by ivy, as if it had made a half-hearted attempt to protect itself from the harsh winter winds. Unlike the castle, whose soft, weathered stone gave the building a certain warmth, the Hunting Lodge looked cold and austere. It was icy and damp inside, even in summer, and turf fires were lit only in the rooms that were going to be used. The many that weren't smelt of mildew and mould.

Kitty's bedroom was on the top floor at the back, with a view of the stables. It was the part of the house referred to as the nursery wing. Victoria, Elspeth and Harry had long since moved into the elegant side near the hall and had large bedrooms overlooking the gardens. Left alone with Miss Grieve, Kitty felt isolated and forgotten.

As she made her way down the narrow corridor to her bedroom she saw the glow of light beneath the door of Miss Grieve's room. She walked on the tips of her toes so as not to draw attention to herself. But as she passed her governess's room she heard the soft sound of weeping. It didn't sound like Miss Grieve at all. She didn't think Miss Grieve had it in her to cry. She stopped outside and pressed her ear to the door. For a moment it occurred to her that Miss Grieve might have a visitor, but Miss Grieve would never break the rules; Kitty's mother did not permit visitors upstairs. Kitty didn't think Miss Grieve had friends anyway. She never spoke of anyone other than her mother who lived in Edinburgh.

Kitty knelt down and put her eye to the keyhole. There, sitting on the bed with a letter lying open in her lap, was Miss Grieve. Kitty was astonished to see her with her brown hair falling in thick curls over her shoulders and down her back. Her face was pale in the lamplight, but her features had softened. She didn't look wooden as she did when she scraped her hair back and drew her lips into a thin line until

144

they almost disappeared. She looked like a sensitive young woman and surprisingly pretty.

Kitty longed to know what the letter said. Had someone died, perhaps Miss Grieve's mother? Her heart swelled with compassion so that she almost turned the knob and let herself in. But Miss Grieve looked so different Kitty felt it might embarrass her to be caught with her guard down. She remained a while transfixed by the trembling mouth, wet with tears, and the dewy skin that seemed to relax away from the bones which usually held it so taut and hard. She was fascinated by Miss Grieve's apparent youth and wondered how old she really was. She had always assumed her to be ancient, but now she wasn't so sure. It was quite possible that she was the same age as Kitty's mother.

After a while Kitty retreated to her bedroom. Nora, one of the housemaids, had lit her small fire and the room smelt pleasantly of smoke. An oil lamp glowed on the chest of drawers against the wall, beneath a picture of garden fairies her grandmother had painted for her. The curtains had been drawn but Kitty opened them wide and sat on the window seat to stare out at the moon and stars that shone brightly in a rich velvet sky.

Kitty did not recognize loneliness because it was so much part of her soul as to blend in seamlessly with the rest of her nature. She felt the familiar tug of something deep and stirring at the bottom of her heart, which always came from gazing out at the beauty of the night, but even though she was aware of a sense of longing she didn't recognize it for what it was – a yearning for love. It was so familiar she had mistaken it for something pleasant and those hours staring into the stars had become as habitual to Kitty as howling at the moon to a craving wolf.

At length Miss Grieve appeared in the doorway, stiff and severe with her hair pulled back into a tight bun, as if she had beaten her emotions into submission and restrained them within her corset. There was no evidence of tears on her rigid cheeks or about her slate-grey eyes and Kitty wondered for a moment whether she had imagined them. What was it that had made Miss Grieve so bitter? 'It's time for your supper, young lady,' she said to Kitty. 'Have you washed your hands?'

Kitty dutifully presented her palms to her governess, who sniffed her disapproval. 'I didn't think so. Go and wash them at once. I don't think it's right for a young lady to be running about the countryside like a stray dog. I'll have a word with your mother. Perhaps piano lessons will be a good discipline for you and keep you out of trouble.'

'Piano lessons have done little for Elspeth,' Kitty replied boldly. 'And when she sings she sounds like a strangled cat.'

'Don't be insolent, Kitty.'

'Victoria sounds even worse when she plays the violin. More like a chorus of strangled cats. I should like to sing.' Kitty poured cold water from the jug into the water bowl and washed her hands with carbolic soap. So far there had been no piano or violin lessons for her, because music was her mother's department and Kitty was invisible to Maud

Deverill. The only reason she had enjoyed riding lessons since the age of two was due to her father's passion for hunting and racing. As long as he lived no child of his would be incompetent in the saddle.

'You're nine now, Kitty, it's about time you learned to make yourself appealing. I don't see why music lessons can't be afforded to you as they are to your sisters. I will speak to your mother tomorrow and see that it is arranged. The less free time you have, the better. The Devil makes work for idle hands.'

Kitty followed Miss Grieve into the nursery where dinner for two was laid up at the table otherwise used for lessons. They stood behind their chairs to say grace and then Miss Grieve sat down while Kitty brought the dish of stew and baked potatoes to the table from the dumb waiter which had been sent up from the kitchen. 'What is it about you that your parents don't wish to see you at mealtimes?' Miss Grieve asked as Kitty sat down. 'I understand from Miss Gibbons that luncheon was always a family affair when your siblings were small.' She helped herself to stew. 'Perhaps it's because you don't yet know how to behave. In my previous position for Lady Billow I always joined the family for luncheon, but I ate my dinner alone, which was a blessed relief. Are we to share this table until you come of age?'

Kitty was used to Miss Grieve's mean jibes and tried not to be riled by them. Wit was her only defence. 'It must be for your pleasure, Miss Grieve, because otherwise you might get lonely.'

Miss Grieve laughed bitterly. 'And I suppose you consider yourself good company, do you?'

'I must be better company than loneliness.'

'I wouldn't be so sure. For a nine-year-old you have an inappropriate tongue. It's no wonder your parents don't wish for the sight of you. Victoria and Elspeth are young ladies, but you, Kitty, are a young ragamuffin in need of taming. That the task should fall to me is a great trial, but I do the best I can out of the goodness of my heart. We've a long way to go before you're in any fit state to find a husband.'

'I don't want a husband,' said Kitty, forking a piece of meat into her mouth. It was cold in the centre.

'Of course you don't want one now. You're a child.'

'Did you ever want a husband, Miss Grieve?'

The governess's eyes shifted a moment uncertainly, revealing more to the sharp little girl than she meant to. 'That's none of your business, Kitty. Sit up straight; you're not a sack of potatoes.'

'Are governesses allowed to marry?' Kitty continued, knowing the answer but enjoying the pained look in Miss Grieve's eyes.

The governess pursed her lips. 'Of course they're allowed to marry. Whatever gave you the idea that they weren't?'

'None of them ever are.' Kitty chewed valiantly on the stringy piece of beef.

'Enough of that lip, my girl, or you can go to bed without any supper.' But Miss Grieve had suddenly gone very pink in the face and Kitty saw a fleeting glimpse of the young woman who had been crying over a letter in her bedroom. She blinked and the image was gone. Miss Grieve was staring into her plate, as if trying hard to control her emotions. Kitty wished she hadn't been so mean but took the opportunity to spit her beef into her napkin and fold it onto her lap without being seen. She tried to think of something nice to say, but nothing came to mind. They sat awhile in silence.

'Do you play the piano, Miss Grieve?' Kitty asked at last.

'I did, once,' she replied tightly.

'Why do you never play?'

The woman glared at Kitty as if she had touched an invisible nerve. 'I've had enough of your questions, young lady. We'll eat the rest of the meal in silence.' Kitty was astonished. She hadn't expected such a harsh reaction to what she felt had been a simple and kind turn of conversation. 'One word and I'll drag you by your red hair and throw you into your bedroom.'

'It's Titian, not red,' Kitty mumbled recklessly.

'You can use all the fancy words you can find, my girl, but red is red and if you ask me, it's very unbecoming.'

Kitty struggled through the rest of dinner in silence. Miss Grieve's face had hardened to granite. Kitty regretted trying to be nice and resolved that she would never be so foolish as to give in to compassion again. When they had finished, Kitty obediently loaded the plates onto the dumb waiter and pressed the bell for it to be pulled down to the kitchen.

She washed with cold water because Sean Doyle, Bridie's brother, who carried hot water upstairs from the kitchen for baths, only did so to the nursery wing every *other* night. Miss Grieve watched over her as she said her prayers. Kitty prayed dutifully for her mama and papa, her siblings and grandparents. Then she added one for Miss Grieve: 'Please, God, take her away. She's horrid and unkind and I hate her. If I knew how to curse like Maggie O'Leary, I'd put one on her so that unhappiness would follow her all the days of her life and never let her go.'

Chapter 3

Maud Deverill sat in the carriage beside her husband in silence. Her gloved hands were folded in the blanket draped over her lap, a fur coat warmed her chest and back but still she shivered. The night was clear and cold and yet a perpetual dampness hung in the air, rising up from the soggy ground, brought inland on the salty sea breeze, assertive enough to penetrate bones. Bertie had returned in the early evening as was his custom, smelling of horse dust and sweat. He had greeted Lady Rowan-Hampton warmly but Maud wasn't fooled by their veneer of respectability. She had often smelt Grace's perfume on his collar and caught the mischievous glances they slipped one another when they thought they weren't being watched. Why, one might ask, did she foster such a close relationship with her husband's mistress? Because she believed, perhaps misguidedly, that it was important to keep one's friends close and one's enemies even closer. So it was with Grace, the most dangerous of all enemies, who she simply couldn't have brought any closer.

The carriage lurched along the farm track that circled the estate, over puddles and holes, until it reached the castle, its passengers quite shaken up. The footman opened the door and offered his hand to Mrs Deverill, who accepted it and put out one uncertain foot, feeling in the dark for the top step. She descended at last and took her husband's arm. Bertie was flaxen-haired and handsome with a wide, well-proportioned face and grey eyes as pale as duck's eggs. He had a dry sense of humour and a penchant for pretty women. Indeed, he was celebrated across Co. Cork for his quiet charm and gentle geniality and was every lady's favourite gentleman, except for Maud's, of course, who resented the fact that he had never really belonged exclusively to her.

Flares had been lit on either side of the castle door to light the way. Bertie and Maud Deverill were the closest neighbours but always the last to arrive on account of Maud's procrastination. She subconsciously hoped that if she dithered and dallied and took her time her husband might go without her.

'If I'm sitting next to the Rector again I shall shoot myself,' she hissed, her scarlet lips black in the darkness.

'My dear, you always sit next to the Rector and you never shoot yourself,' Bertie replied patiently.

'Your mother does it on purpose to spite me.'

'Now why would she do that?'

'Because she despises me.'

'Nonsense. Mama despises no one. The two of you are simply very different. I don't see why you can't get along.'

'I have a headache. I should not have come at all.'

'Since you are here, you might as well enjoy yourself.'

'It's all right for you, Bertie. You're always the life and soul of the party. Everyone loves *you*. I'm just here to facilitate your pleasure.'

'Don't be absurd, Maud. Come along, you'll catch your death out here. I need a drink.' They stepped into the hall and Maud reluctantly peeled off her fur coat and gloves and handed them to O'Flynn.

Maud was a beautiful, if severe-looking, woman. She was blessed with high cheekbones, a symmetrical heart-shaped face, large pale-blue eyes and a pretty, straight nose. Her mouth was full-lipped and her blonde hair thick and lustrous, pinned up in the typical Edwardian style with curls and waves in all the right places. Her skin was milky white, her hands and feet dainty. In fact, she was like a lovely marble statue, carved by a benevolent creator, yet cold and hard and lacking in all sensuality. The only quality that gave her an ounce of character was her inability to see beyond herself.

Tonight she wore a pale blue dress that reached the floor and showed off her slender figure, a pearl choker about her neck with a diamond clasp glittering at her throat. When she entered the drawing room there was a collective gasp of admiration, which cheered her up enormously. She glided in, feeling much better about the evening, and found herself accosted at once by Adeline's eccentric spinster sisters Hazel and Laurel.

'My dear Maud, you look lovely,' gushed Hazel. 'Don't you think, Laurel? Maud looks lovely.'

Laurel, who was rarely far from her sister's side, smiled into her chubby crimson cheeks. 'She does, Hazel. She truly does. Simply lovely.' Maud looked down her nose at the two round faces grinning eagerly up at her and smiled politely, before extricating herself as quickly as possible with the excuse of going to greet the Rector. 'Poor Mrs Daunt has taken a turn,' said Hazel of the Rector's wife.

'We shall ask Mary to bake a cake tomorrow and take it round,' suggested Laurel, referring to their maid.

'Splendid idea, Hazel. A little brandy in it should restore her to health, don't you think?'

'Oh, it will indeed!' exclaimed the ever-exuberant Laurel, clapping her small hands excitedly.

The Rector was a portly, self-important man with a long prickly moustache and bloated, ruddy cheeks, who enjoyed life's pleasures as if the obligation to do so was one of God's lesser-known Commandments. He hunted with gusto, was a fine shot and a keen fisherman. Often seen waddling among his flock at the races, he never missed the opportunity to preach, as if his constant moralizing justified his presence there in that den of iniquity. Maud was a religious woman, when it suited her, and she abhorred the Rector for his flamboyance. The vicar in her home town in England had been an austere, simple man of austere and simple pleasures, which was how she believed all religious men should be. But she held out her hand and greeted him, disguising her true feelings behind a veneer of cool politeness. 'Well if it isn't the lovely Mrs Deverill,' he said, taking her slender hand in his spongy one and giving it a hearty shake. 'Did Victoria get the reading for tomorrow's service?' he asked.

'Yes, she did,' Maud replied. 'I've practised with her but you know young people, they read much too quickly.'

'I understand she will soon be leaving us for London.'

'I don't know how I shall make do without her,' said Maud, who always managed to swing every conversation round to herself. 'I shall be quite bereft with only Elspeth for company.'

'You will soon have Harry back for the holidays and of course you still have—' He was about to mention Kitty but Maud cut him off briskly.

'One pays a heavy price for a good education,' she said solemnly. 'But it is the way of the world and Harry is happy at Eton so I shouldn't complain. I miss him terribly. He is worth ten of my daughters. God didn't see fit to give me more sons,' she added reproachfully, as if the Rector were somehow responsible.

'Your daughters will look after you in old age,' said the Rector helpfully, draining his glass of sherry.

'Harry will look after me in my old age. My daughters will be much too busy with their own children to think about me.'

At that moment Adeline joined them, her sweet smile and twinkling eyes giving the Rector a warm feeling of relief. 'We were just saying, Lady Deverill, how daughters are great comforts to their mothers in old age.'

'I wouldn't know, my daughter having crossed the Atlantic without a backward glance,' said Adeline, not unkindly. 'But I'm sure you're right. Maud is quite spoiled with three daughters.' Maud averted her eyes. Adeline had an unsettling way of looking right through her as if she recognized her shortcomings for what they were and was even slightly amused by them.

'There's a good chance Victoria and Elspeth will marry Englishmen and leave Ireland altogether. My hope lies with Harry for, whomever he weds, he will live here.'

Adeline looked steadily at Maud. 'You're forgetting Kitty, my dear.'

The Rector grinned broadly, for he was very fond of the youngest Deverill. 'Now *she* won't be leaving Ireland, not Kitty. I'd put a lot of money on her marrying an Irishman.' Maud tried to smile but her crimson lips could only manage a grimace.

Adeline shook her head, her special affection for Kitty undisguised. 'She's quite fearless. She'll do something surprising, for certain. I'd put good money on *that*.' Maud felt she was expected to add something to the conversation, but she didn't really know what her daughter was like. Only that she had the same flame-red hair as Adeline and the same unsettling knowing in her eyes.

At last O'Flynn appeared in the doorway to announce that dinner was now ready. Maud found her husband discussing the next hunt meeting with his father, who was already on his third glass of sherry. Lord Deverill always managed to look moth-eaten. His grey hair was wild, as if he had just arrived at a gallop, and his dinner jacket looked as if it had been nibbled at the elbows by mice. As hard as Skiddy tried to keep his master's clothes clean and pressed, they still appeared to have been pulled out of the bottom of a drawer – and he refused, doggedly, to buy new clothes, ever. 'May I have the pleasure of escorting you in to dinner, Maud?' Hubert asked, taking pleasure from her beautiful face. Maud, who could always rely on her father-in-law's support, slipped her hand under his arm and allowed him to lead her into the dining room.

Bertie escorted the Shrubs on either arm, allowing their excited chatter to rise above him like the unobtrusive twittering of birds. The Rector walked in with Adeline, their conversation having been reduced to a one-sided lecture by him on women's suffrage, to which Adeline listened with half an ear and even less interest.

They stood to say grace, Hubert at the head, Adeline at the foot, with the Rector on Adeline's right side, next to a furious Maud. They bowed their heads and the Rector spoke in the low, portentous voice of the pulpit. The moment it was over the door burst open and Rupert, Bertie's younger brother, stood dishevelled and obviously drunk with his hands on the door frame. 'Is there a place for me?' he asked, appealing to his mother.

Adeline didn't look at all surprised to see her middle child, who lived in the house previously occupied by her late mother-in-law, the Dowager Lady Deverill, a mile or so across the fields, overlooking the sea. 'Why don't you sit between your aunts,' she said, sinking into her chair.

Hubert, who had less patience for his hopeless son and believed he would have done better to have joined his younger sister in America, found a wife and perhaps made something of his life, gave a loud 'Harrumph' and said, 'Cook's day off, is it?'

Rupert smiled with all his charm. 'I heard my dear aunts Hazel and Laurel were coming for dinner, Papa, and I couldn't resist.' The Shrubs blushed with pleasure, unaware of his slightly mocking tone, and moved apart so O'Flynn could slip a chair between them.

'What a delightful evening this has turned out to be,' gushed Laurel. 'Don't you think, Hazel?'

'Oh, I most certainly do, Laurel. Come and sit down, Rupert my dear, and tell us what you have been up to. You lead such an exciting life, doesn't he? In fact, we were only saying yesterday what it must be to be young, weren't we, Laurel?'

'Oh yes, we were. We're so old, Hazel and I, that all we can do is enjoy the little titbits you give us, Rupert, like crumbs from the rich man's table.'

Rupert sat down and unfolded his napkin. 'What has Mrs Doyle cooked up for us this evening?' he said.

*

158

It was past midnight when Bertie and Maud drove back to the Hunting Lodge. Maud vented her fury to her weary and pleasantly tipsy husband. 'Rupert is a disgrace, turning up uninvited like that. He was smashed, too, and poorly dressed. You'd have thought he'd have the decency to dress properly for dinner, considering the amount of money your father lavishes on him.' She fell forward as the carriage went over a pothole.

'Mama and Papa don't care about that sort of thing,' he replied with a yawn.

'They should care. Civilization is about standards. This country would descend into barbarism if it wasn't for people like us keeping the standards up. Appearances matter, Bertie. Your parents should set an example.'

'Are you suggesting they're poorly dressed, Maud?'

'Your father's eaten by moths. What harm would it do to go to London and visit his tailor once in a while?'

'He's got more important things to think about.'

'Like hunting, shooting and fishing, I suppose?'

'Quite so. He is old. Leave him to his pleasure.'

'As for your aunts, they're ridiculous.'

'They're happy and good and kind. You're a harsh judge of people, Maud. Is there no one you like?'

'Rupert needs a wife,' she added, changing the subject.

'Then find him one.'

'He should go to London and look for a nice English girl with good manners and a firm hand to smack him into shape.'

'You're bitter, Maud. Was tonight really so bad?'

'Oh, you had a splendid time in the dining room, drinking port and smoking cigars, while we languished in the drawing room. Do you know, your mother and her sisters are going to hold a séance here at the castle? They're a trio of witches. It's absurd.'

'Oh, leave them to their fun, my dear. How does it affect you if they want to communicate with the dead?'

Maud realized her argument was weak. 'It's ungodly,' she added tartly. 'I don't imagine the Rector would think much of their game – no good will come of it, mark my words.'

'I still don't see how it affects *you*, Maud.'

'Your mother is a bad influence on Kitty,' she rejoined, knowing that Kitty's name would carry more weight.

Bertie frowned and rubbed his bristly chin. 'Ah Kitty,' he sighed, feeling a stab of guilt.

'She spends much too much time talking nonsense with her grandmother.'

'Might that be because *you* don't spend any time with her at all?'

Maud sat in silence for a while, affronted. Bertie had never complained before about her obvious lack of interest in their youngest. Besides, it was customary that young children should be kept out of sight and in the nursery with their governesses. Then it came to her in a sudden flood of pain: Grace Rowan-Hampton must have mentioned it to him. By keeping her enemy close she had allowed a spy into her home.

The carriage drew up in front of the Hunting Lodge and stopped outside the front door. It was lightly drizzling, what the locals called 'soft rain'. A strong wind swept over the land, moaning eerily as it dashed through the bare branches of the horse chestnut trees. The butler was waiting for them in the hall with an oil lamp to light their way upstairs. Feeling more discontented than ever, Maud followed her husband up to the landing, hoping he would notice her silence and ask what was troubling her. 'Goodnight, my dear,' he said, without so much as a glance. She watched him disappear into his room and close the door behind him. Furiously she went into hers, where her lady's maid was waiting to unhook her dress. Without a word she turned her back expectantly.

The following morning Kitty breakfasted with Miss Grieve in the nursery then dressed for church. The Sunday service, in the church of St Patrick in Ballinakelly, was the only time the family all gathered together. The only time Kitty really saw her parents. Miss Grieve had put out a fresh white pinafore and polished black boots and spent much longer than necessary combing the knots out of her hair without any consideration for the pain she caused. But Kitty fixed her stare on the grey clouds scudding across the sky outside the window and willed herself not to shed a single tear.

While her parents and grandparents rode in carriages, Kitty and her sisters sat in the pony and trap with Miss Grieve in the front beside Mr Mills, who held the reins.

Victoria was pretty like her mother with a wide, heart-shaped face, a long, straight nose and shrewish blue eyes. Her blonde hair fell down to her waist in lustrous curls as she sat with her back straight and her chin up, much too aware of her own beauty and the admiring looks it aroused. Elspeth was more modest and less attractive than her elder sister. Her hair was mouse-brown, her nose a fleshy button, her expression as submissive and dim-witted as a lap dog's. The older girls ignored Kitty completely, preferring to talk to each other. But Kitty didn't mind: she was much too busy looking around at the fields of cows and sheep.

'Mother says I have to have new dresses made for London,' said Victoria happily, holding her hat so it didn't fly off in the wind. 'She has already sent my measurements to Cousin Beatrice. I can hardly wait. They'll be the most fashionable designs for sure.'

'You're so lucky,' said Elspeth, who had a tendency to elongate her vowels so that her voice sounded like a whine. 'I wish I were coming with you. Instead I'm going to be all alone with no one to talk to but Mama. It's going to be frightfully dull without you.'

'You had better get used to it, Elspeth,' said her sister sharply. 'I fully intend to find a husband.'

'That's what it's all for, I suppose.'

'Mama told me that if one doesn't find a husband it is because one is ugly, dull or both.'

'You are neither ugly nor dull,' said Elspeth. 'Fortunately neither of us inherited Grandma's ginger hair.'

'It's not ginger,' interrupted Kitty from beneath her bonnet. 'It's Titian red.'

Her sisters giggled. 'Mama says it's ginger,' said Victoria meanly.

'It's very unlucky to have red hair,' Elspeth added. 'Fishermen will head for home if they see a red-haired woman on the way to their boats. Clodagh told me,' she said, referring to one of the maids.

'You'd better keep it under that bonnet of yours then,' said Victoria. She looked down at her youngest sister and Kitty lifted her grey eyes and stared at her boldly. Victoria stopped laughing and grew suddenly afraid. There was something scary in her sister's gaze, as if she could cast a spell just by looking at someone. 'Let's not be unkind,' she said uneasily, not wanting to incite Kitty's wrath in case she somehow jinxed her first London season. 'Red hair is all right if it's combined with a pretty face, isn't that so, Elspeth?' She dug her elbow into her sister's ribs.

'Yes, it is,' Elspeth agreed dutifully. But Kitty was no longer listening. She was watching the local Catholic children walking back from Mass, looking for Bridie and Jack O'Leary.

Chapter 4

Ballinakelly was a quaint town of pretty white houses that clustered on the hillside like mussels on a rock, all the way down to the sea. There was a small harbour, three churches (St Patrick's, Church of Ireland, the Methodist church and the Catholic church of All Saints), a high street of little shops and four public houses, which were always full. The local children attended the school, which was run by the Catholic church, and gathered at the shrine to the Virgin Mary most evenings to witness the statue swaying, which it very often did, apparently all on its own. Built into the hillside in 1828 to commemorate a young girl's vision, it had become something of a tourist attraction in the summer months as pilgrims travelled from far and wide to see it, falling to their knees in the mud and crossing themselves devoutly when it duly rattled. The children were greatly amused by the spectacle, running off in their pack of scruffy scamps, hiding their fear beneath peals of nervous laughter. It was whispered that horses sometimes baulked when passing it, foretelling a tragedy.

The pony and trap made its way slowly through the town. Kitty eagerly searched the rabble of Catholic children walking towards her. They were pale with hunger, having fasted from the evening before, and dazed with boredom from the service. At last she saw Bridie, treading heavily up the street with her family. Her face, half-hidden behind a tangle of knotted hair, was grim. Kitty knew she didn't like going to Mass. Father Quinn was a severe and unforgiving priest, prone to outbursts of indignation in the pulpit and quite often reproachful finger-wagging as he picked on members of the congregation whom he felt had, in some way, transgressed. The poorest among them received the worst of his tongue-lashing.

Kitty focused hard on her friend until Bridie raised her eyes and saw her, just as the pony and trap clip-clopped past. Bridie's face lit up and she smiled. Kitty smiled back. A little behind Bridie, Liam O'Leary, the vet, walked beside his twelve-year-old son, Jack. Kitty smiled at him, too. Jack was more discreet. His blue eyes twinkled beneath his thick brown fringe and the corners of his mouth gave a tiny twitch. The pony walked on. When Kitty looked back she caught eyes with him again as he tossed her another furtive glance over his shoulder.

The church of St Patrick was almost full. Here the aristocracy came together with the ordinary working-class Protestants – shopkeepers, cattle jobbers, dressmakers and the Castle Deverill estate manager and bookkeeper, all descended from the Huguenots. Lord and Lady Deverill sat in the front pew with Bertie, Maud, Victoria and Elspeth. Miss Grieve sat in the row behind with Kitty. Much to Kitty's delight she found herself sitting next to Lady Rowan-Hampton, wrapped snugly in a warm coat and fur stole. Her husband, the portly and red-faced Sir Ronald, had to sit on the aisle side in order to get out to read the lesson. 'My dear Kitty,' whispered Lady Rowan-Hampton happily, placing her prayer book on the ledge in front of her. 'I haven't seen you for such a long time. Haven't you grown into a pretty girl? I must say, you've inherited your grandmother's good looks. You know, as a young woman her beauty was the talk of Dublin. Now, how are we to get through the service? I know, let's play a game. Find an animal that matches each member of your family, and Reverend Daunt, of course, let's not forget him. If you were an animal, Kitty, you'd be ... ' She narrowed her soft brown eyes and Kitty was transfixed by her rosy cheeks, slightly on the plump side, her smooth powdery skin and full, expressive mouth. Kitty thought that, if people were cakes, Lady Rowan-Hampton would be a juicy Victoria sponge cake, whereas her mother would be a dry and bitter porter cake. 'Of course, my dear, you'd be a fox!' Lady Rowan-Hampton continued. 'You'd be a very cunning and charming little fox.'

The service began with the first hymn and Kitty stood tall and sang as prettily as she could in order to impress Lady Rowan-Hampton. Miss Grieve just mouthed the words, Kitty supposed, because her voice was inaudible. Mrs Daunt, the Rector's wife, usually played the organ, almost as badly as Elspeth played the piano, but today, as Mrs Daunt was indisposed, their neighbour, the porcine Mr Rowe, played the violin beautifully. Kitty could smell Lady Rowan-Hampton's perfume, which was floral and very sweet, like tuberose, and Kitty decided that when she was grown-up she wanted to be just like her. Of course, she didn't want a fat old husband like Sir Ronald, who was Master of the local hunt, a loud bore and contrary when drunk – Kitty had often heard him holding forth in the dining room after dinner when the women had gone through to the drawing room. Lady Rowan-Hampton always wore glittering diamonds about her neck and wrists and long dresses that swished as she walked. She was the closest thing to a princess that Kitty had ever seen. Now she was sitting beside her, Kitty was more enthralled than ever.

Sir Ronald read the first lesson. His booming voice rebounded off the walls as he threw each syllable into the congregation as if he were a colonel lobbing grenades. Victoria read the second, softly and a little too fast, swallowing the ends of the sentences so their meaning was almost entirely lost. As Reverend Daunt warmed to his sermon, Lady Rowan-Hampton leaned down and whispered a word into Kitty's ear. 'Walrus.' Kitty stifled a giggle, because *that* was the very animal Kitty had thought of when Sir Ronald had read the lesson.

During the final hymn the collection plate was passed

round. Lady Rowan-Hampton handed Kitty a coin so that, when the plate reached her, she was able to drop it in among the others with a light clink. At the end of the service Mr Rowe took up his violin and played a jig, which made most people smile in amusement, except for Maud whose tight lips pursed even tighter with disapproval. 'So, what animal do you think your father would be?' Lady Rowan-Hampton asked Kitty.

'A lion,' said Kitty.

'Very good,' said Lady Rowan-Hampton approvingly. 'I think you're right. He's fair and handsome, just like a lion. And your mama?'

'A white weasel.'

Lady Rowan-Hampton was shocked. 'My dear, are you sure you know what a weasel looks like?'

'Of course. Don't you think she looks just like one?'

Lady Rowan-Hampton hesitated and flushed. 'Not really. I think she's more like a lovely snow leopard.' Kitty crinkled her nose and thought of the dry porter cake. 'Your sisters?'

Lady Rowan-Hampton asked.

'*Little* weasels,' said Kitty with a grin.

'Oh dear, a very weaselly lot,' said Lady Rowan-Hampton, smiling too. 'I think we should keep this game to ourselves, don't you think?' Kitty nodded and watched the weasels get up and file down the aisle towards the door.

Once out in the sunshine, the congregation took the opportunity to mingle. The Anglo-Irish, being such a small community, had known each other for generations and cleaved to each other for comfort and safety. They hunted together, met at the races and enjoyed an endless circuit of hunt balls and dinner parties. They were united by a love of sport and entertainment, a loyalty to the Crown, a wary respect for the Irish and a subliminal determination to keep going in a changing world as if their decline as a people were not inevitable.

Kitty found a spider's web studded with raindrops on the grass not far from where her father was now talking to Lady Rowan-Hampton. Sensing they were discussing *her*, she turned her attention away from the spider to see if she could work out what they were saying. Once or twice her father glanced in her direction and she had to pretend she was looking elsewhere. Lady Rowan-Hampton was gesticulating in a persuasive manner, and quite crossly too, by the way she vigorously moved her hands. Kitty was surprised to see her father so contrite, as if he was being told off. Then Kitty was diverted by another pair of eyes that watched the couple from the opposite end of the yard. They belonged to her mother and they were colder than ever.

Sunday lunch was always held up at the castle. The family gathered in the drawing room by a boisterous fire, to warm up after the freezing-cold church and blustery ride back with glasses of sherry and large tumblers of Jameson's whiskey. The Shrubs were always included, arriving in a trap with the ribbons of their hats flapping madly in the wind and their heads pressed together, deep in conversation.

Rupert always came alone, already tipsy, and charmed his parents' other guests who often increased the number around the table to as many as twenty. Today, it was just the family, however, and Kitty sat at the very end of the table, beside her sisters, who ignored her. To her surprise, her father addressed her.

'Kitty, my dear, come and ride with me this afternoon. I'd like to see how you're coming along.' Elspeth turned and glared at her in surprise. It was a rare treat to be asked to ride with their father. 'It's about time you rode with the grown-ups, eh? No more languishing in the nursery for you, my girl. How old are you now, eight?'

'Nine,' said Kitty.

'Nine, eh? Where's the time gone? When I was nearly half your age I was hunting with the Ballinakelly Foxhounds.'

'What fun!' exclaimed Hazel.

'Yes, indeed,' agreed Laurel. 'Do take care to find her a gentle pony, Bertie. When I was a girl I barely escaped with my life after being thrown into a ditch by my naughty little pony, Teasel. Do you remember, Hazel?'

'Do I ever!' laughed her sister. Hubert immediately launched into his favourite hunting anecdote and Kitty was quite lost again in the sudden swell of conversation. But her heart began to thump excitely at the thought of riding out with her father. She wondered whether her mother would come too, but decided not. After all, this impromptu arrangement was clearly Lady Rowan-Hampton's idea and her mother rarely rode. When she did she cut a dash in her black riding habit and hat with its diaphanous black veil reaching down to her chin.

Kitty loved to ride. She adored the wild and rugged hills, the birds of prey that hovered overhead, the gurgling streams and swelling sea. She was curious about the world outside her own isolated existence and liked nothing more than to escape whenever the opportunity arose. Now she set off with her father at a gentle pace, he on his tall chestnut horse, she on a small grey pony called Thruppence. 'Where are we going?' she asked, as they walked up the long avenue of tall, leafless trees.

'Where would you like to go?' her father replied, looking down at her with kind, smiling eyes.

'To the Fairy Ring,' Kitty replied.

Bertie arched an eyebrow. He knew it well but the place held no interest for him. 'If that's what you want.'

'I ride there with Grandma.'

'I bet you do.' He laughed. 'Do you dance among the stones when there's a full moon?'

'Of course,' she replied seriously. 'We turn into wolves and howl.'

Bertie stared at her in astonishment. His daughter held his gaze for a long moment with her unsettling grey eyes, then her face broke into a grin and Bertie realized, to his relief, that she was joking. 'What a sense of humour you have for an eight-year-old.'

171

'Nine,' Kitty said emphatically.

He shook his head and thought how irregular it was for such a young child to be so unnaturally grown-up. Grace had been right to berate him. It wasn't fitting for his youngest to languish alone in the nursery with her austere Scottish governess. He knew full well that Maud had no interest in the child, but he hadn't bothered to find out the extent of her neglect. Now he felt guilty. He should have intervened earlier. 'You're a weak man,' Grace had scolded him and her words had stung. 'Your aversion to confrontation has meant that Maud has been allowed to do as she pleases. Now take charge, Bertie, and *do* something about it.'

'Then let's go to the Fairy Ring and you can show me what you and Mother get up to when you're alone together,' he said, and the smile Kitty gave him made him wonder why he didn't seek her company more often.

The Fairy Ring was an ancient and mystical formation of seventeen large grey rocks positioned on the summit of a hill, overlooking the patchwork of fields that stretched all the way to the ocean. From up there they could see cottages shivering in the dusk, thin ribbons of smoke rising from their chimneys as the farmers' families huddled by their turf fires to keep warm.

'All this is Deverill land,' said Bertie, sweeping his eyes over the vast acres of farmland. 'We had ten times as much before the Wyndham Act enabled tenants to buy their own land. We've lived well for over two hundred years, but life as we know it will one day come to an end as our diminishing estates will no longer be able to support our lifestyle. I don't suppose Miss Grieve has taught you anything about *that*.' Kitty shook her head. Her father had no idea how to talk to a nine-year-old. 'No, I didn't think so,' said Bertie dolefully. 'What does she teach you?'

'The Great Fire of London and the Plague.'

'It's time you learned about your own heritage.'

'Barton Deverill?' she said eagerly.

Her father smiled. 'You already know about him. Of course you should know about your ancestors, but you should also know about the Irish nationalists' struggle for independence, Kitty. The Irish people don't want to be ruled by the British. They want to govern themselves.'

'I know about that,' she said, remembering what Bridie had told her. 'They hate that the British have all the power and the taxes are too high.'

He raised his eyebrows in surprise. 'So you know something already?'

She knew not to reveal that she played with the Catholic children and listened to their patriotic chatter. 'I know that the Irish don't like us, even though we are Irish too.'

'We're *Anglo*-Irish, Kitty.'

'I'm not,' she said defiantly, folding her arms. 'I don't like England.'

'It's England that enabled you to live here. If it wasn't for Charles II Barton Deverill would never have been given these lands in the first place.'

'They belonged to the O'Learys,' she said boldly.

Bertie narrowed his eyes and thought a moment before replying, as if working out the best way to be tactful. 'The land he built the castle on was indeed O'Leary land.'

'Do they want it back?'

'I'm sure they did at the time, Kitty. But that all happened over two hundred years ago. Liam O'Leary is a vet, as was his father before him. They haven't been farmers for generations.'

'So, there's no fighting then?'

'No fighting, no.'

'Then you're friends?'

He shuffled uneasily on his horse, thinking of Liam's resentful wife. 'Quite friendly, yes.'

'Then there's the possibility that a Deverill might one day marry an O'Leary, after all?'

'I think that's highly unlikely,' Bertie replied tightly. 'You've been listening to your grandmother, haven't you? Her stories are great fun, Kitty, but it's important that you understand that they are just fun and not real. They're like Greek myths and Irish legends like "The Children of Lir", to be enjoyed but not taken literally. So, what do you and Grandma do here?' He pointed his riding crop at the rocks.

'This was an ancient place of worship for pagans,' said Kitty confidently. 'Each one of these stones is a person cursed to live as stone by day. When the sun sets they come alive.'

'Very interesting,' said Bertie, not in the least interested

174

in magic. He turned his mind to the bottle of gin and the cheery fire that awaited him on his return.

'Don't you want to see it?' Kitty turned her face to the sun. It was already melting into the sea on the horizon and setting the sky aflame with rich reds and golds.

'Another time,' he replied patiently, realizing that even Maud had a point when she complained that Kitty was spending too much time talking nonsense with her grandmother.

They set off back down the hill. The evening was cold, but rich smells of damp soil and heather rose up from the sodden ground to infuse the February air with the promise of spring. Occasionally a partridge or a hare bolted out of the gorse as they passed, and a herd of cows came close to watch them with their big brown eyes and placid mooing. Kitty delighted in them all, wishing she could stay out for longer and not have to return to the dull nursery wing to dine alone with Miss Grieve. But when she got back to her room Miss Grieve was there, in her stiff dress that left only her pale face and hands exposed, to inform her that she was expected at the dinner table tonight.

'I can't imagine why they want you all of a sudden,' said Miss Grieve reproachfully. 'After all, up until now they've barely noticed your existence.'

'It's because I'm nine and Papa thought I was eight,' Kitty replied. 'Silly Papa.'

'I hope you mind your manners. I won't be there to prod you.'

'I don't need any prodding, Miss Grieve. I shall behave like a young lady.'

'Don't get above yourself, my girl. You're not a young lady yet. So, where did you go with your father?'

Kitty knew not to mention the Fairy Ring. Once, on a wave of enthusiasm, she had told Miss Grieve that she had seen the stones come to life, only to receive a good walloping on the palms of her hands with the riding crop. She wouldn't forget herself so quickly again. 'We rode up on the hills. It was delightful.'

'Well, don't get too used to it. I don't suppose he'll ask you again. I think he must prefer the company of Miss Victoria; after all, she's a young woman now. Oh, she'll be off to London in the spring and that'll be the last we'll see of her, I don't doubt. She'll find herself a nice husband, a pretty girl like her. Then it'll be Miss Elspeth's turn and she'll be away like the wind. As for you . . . ' Miss Grieve looked down her long nose at Kitty. 'A poor little thing like you. You'll be lucky to be as fortunate as your sisters with all your disadvantages. Don't look at me like that. Screwing your face up makes you even less attractive.'

Kitty stepped into her best dress and clenched her fists as Miss Grieve pulled the knots out of her hair. 'If I had my say I'd cut it off altogether,' she said, tugging on a particularly sensitive tendril of hair at Kitty's temple. 'The lengths we go to when the simplest solution would be a pair of scissors!'

When Kitty was ready she ran downstairs, leaving Miss Grieve to eat alone in the nursery with only her sourness for company. She stopped in front of the mirror on the landing and stared at her reflection. Was she really so ugly? Had Lady Rowan-Hampton simply been kind when she had complimented her looks? And, if she was so unattractive, did it really matter? Then she thought of her grandmother and smiled. She was a beautiful soul of God; Miss Grieve was just too blind to see it.

Chapter 5

It was Sunday night. Old Mrs Nagle's turf fire was smoking heavily as she puffed on a clay pipe and fingered her rosary devoutly. A big black bastible full of parsnip and potato stew was suspended above it, throwing out steam into the already smoggy atmosphere. She sat in her usual chair beside the fire, a hunched and emaciated figure dressed in black, chewing on her gums for her teeth had fallen out long ago. Her granddaughter, Bridie, dutifully stirred the stew with a wooden spoon as her stomach groaned like a hungry dog at the rich, salty smell. Mrs Doyle sat in her rocking chair opposite her mother, half listening to her husband and sons, the rest of her attention focused on her basket of darning. Bridie's two elder brothers, Michael and Sean, sat with their father around the wooden table talking in low voices, their serious faces distorted in the flickering candlelight that burned through the gloom, their rough labourers' hands clutching pewter tumblers of Beamish stout. Every now and then Bridie caught something of what they were

178

saying. But she'd heard it many times before. Talk of Fenian uprisings against the British, worry about working for the aristocracy, always the concern that they might be seen as spies or traitors, and then what?

Bridie had long been aware of the Irish struggle for independence, and the resentment of the British. She had heard talk of it wafting up through the floorboards with the scent of porter and tobacco as she drifted off to sleep, her father and his friends discussing it long into the night, their voices loud and unguarded as they drank and played cards. She had seen copies of the Sinn Féin newspaper lying hidden beneath Michael's bed but struggled to read them. Her father, Tomas Doyle, was a wise man when sober. He would argue that Lord Deverill was a beneficent landlord, unlike many, and Sean as well as Mrs Doyle were employed up at the castle and treated kindly. Wasn't it true that during the great potato famine the previous Lady Deverill had set up a soup kitchen in one of the hay barns and saved many from starvation? It was well known that not one of the Deverill tenants had died of hunger during the famine, or taken the coffin ship to Amerikey, thanks be to God. But Michael, Bridie's oldest brother, who was nearly nineteen now and worked with his father on the land, wanted the British Protestants out, whoever they were and however good they were to their tenants. It was a matter of principle and honour: Ireland should belong to the Irish, he maintained passionately, and the British 'Prods' should go back to England where they belonged. 'A privilege to buy our land? What privilege is it to buy back land that was stolen from us in the first place?' he would maintain, banging his fist on the table, his long black hair falling over his forehead. 'They've stolen more than land. They've stolen our culture, our history, our language and our way of life.' Bridie would hear their voices grow louder as they each tried to persuade the other and she would feel anxious for Kitty and for their secret friendship, which she so treasured. She hoped that if ever there was trouble in Ballinakelly, the Deverills would not suffer at the hands of the rebels on account of their well-known generosity and kindness towards the local people.

Bridie was disappointed Kitty hadn't come to see her today. Usually she'd find Kitty sitting on the wall surrounding the castle grounds and they'd run off together and play pikki with the local children. Kitty called it hopscotch but she played it all the same. Kitty was like that; if it was fun she'd throw herself into the game with all her heart and not give a thought to whether she should or should not mix with the Catholic children. She didn't care either whether one of those children was an O'Leary.

When Bridie thought of Jack O'Leary, with his idle gaze and his pet hawk on his arm, something tickled her belly, like the soft fluttering of butterfly wings. Jack was lofty and handsome with thick brown hair and eyes as watery blue as an Irish sky in winter. An arrogant smirk played about his lips and there was always a mocking laughter in those wintry eyes as he watched the girls at their childish play. But

Jack had a sensitive side too. He loved all God's creatures, from the secretive spider to the docile donkey, and spent most of his time among them. He'd lie on his stomach in the early evening and wait for badgers, leave out food for stray dogs and birdwatch down on the beach in Smuggler's Bay. He'd taken Kitty and Bridie along one afternoon in January to watch a family of mice in the garden shed behind his house. They'd stayed for over an hour, as still as statues, as the mice had scampered about the wooden floor as if on tiny wheels, eating the seed Jack had put out for them. That small episode had bonded them like plotters in a conspiracy, and from that moment on they had set out together for more adventures in the wild. Kitty was bold and unafraid, curious about all the creatures Jack showed them, but Bridie was scared of creepy-crawlies and hairy mollies and sometimes needed coaxing. Jack would laugh at her apprehension and say, 'All animals are the goodies if you see life from their point of view, even the smelly rat. Indeed they all have a God-given right to be on this earth.' And Jack would tell them about life from the rat's point of view and Bridie would try hard to be sympathetic.

Today Jack hadn't come out either. His father, Liam O'Leary the vet, had begun to take him along when he went to examine colicky horses, lame sheep, and dogs wounded in fights. There was plenty of work for a vet in a place full of animals like Ballinakelly. So, Bridie had spent the day with the other children whom she didn't like as much as Kitty nor admire as much as Jack.

181

Bridie loved Kitty like the sister she had never had, but she did wonder sometimes if the girl wasn't a bit 'quare' with her talk of ghosts. Perhaps she was driven to make-believe because she was so lonely hidden away in the nursery with only the grim Miss Grieve for company. Bridie shuddered to think that those ghosts might be real. 'Don't ye be forgetting to stir, Bridie,' said her mother sharply, looking up from her sewing. Bridie hadn't noticed her hand had stopped and sat up with a jolt.

'She's away with the fairies,' Old Mrs Nagle tutted, shaking her head. Bridie didn't think her grandmother would say that about *her* if she knew some of the things Kitty said.

After tea Mrs Doyle announced it was time for prayer and Bridie knelt on the floor with her father and brothers, as she did every evening, elbows on the chair, fingers knitted, head bowed. Old Mrs Nagle remained seated in her chair and mumbled the words of the prayer through toothless gums. 'Thou oh Lord will open my lips,' said Mrs Doyle solemnly.

'And my tongue shall announce thy praise,' they all responded. Then Mrs Doyle recited the prayer she knew so well it might have been embossed on her heart. The tail ends were short: a hasty prayer for friends and family and for Lord and Lady Deverill, who were both benevolent and fair.

After prayers the neighbours descended on the cottage, as they always did, with their fiddles and Old Badger Hanratty's illegal poteen, distilled from potatoes in a disguised hay rick outside his cottage and of a surprisingly high quality. It wasn't long before the singing began. Bridie loved to sit with her buttermilk, listening to the Irish folk songs and watching the sentimental old men reduced to tears as they wallowed in nostalgia. Sometimes they'd dance the 'Siege of Ennis' and her mother would shout, 'Off ye go, lads, twice round the kitchen, and for God's sake mind the dresser.' Or her father would grab her mother and they'd dance to the foot-stamping and table-banging, round and round, until Mrs Doyle's red face glowed with pleasure and she looked like a young girl being courted by an overzealous suitor.

Bridie's father was rough with coarse black hair and a thick black beard and she doubted she would recognize him if he returned home one day clean-shaven. He was short but as strong as a bull, and woe betide anyone who dared take him on in a fight. He'd won many a pub brawl and broken countless jaws and teeth in the process. He was quick to temper but just as quick to repent and the few times he'd struck his sons he'd fallen to his knees in a heap of regret, crossing himself profusely and promising the Holy Virgin Mary not to do it again. Drink was his curse but a good heart his blessing; it was simply a matter of finding a balance between the two.

Suddenly her father weaved his way across the room towards her. She expected him to send her up to bed, but instead he took her hand and said, 'Indeed and I'll be dan cing with my Bridie tonight.' And he pulled her to her feet.

Embarrassed that everyone was watching, she blushed the colour of a berry. But she needn't have worried about the steps; she had seen the older girls dancing often enough. Her father swung her round and round the kitchen just like he did Mrs Doyle, and as she was swung she saw a sea of smiles and among them was her mother's, a tender look softening the work-weary contours of her face. After that her brothers took turns and Bridie, so often the spectator, became the focus of their attention and her heart swelled with pleasure.

That night Bridie could barely sleep for excitement. Her mind had drifted during the recital of the rosary because it had been such a joyous evening. She didn't imagine Kitty had evenings like that, dancing with her father, and she rarely saw her brother who was at school in England. For a moment Bridie gave in to the superior feeling. She bathed in it, allowing her envy to be eclipsed by a warm sense of supremacy. She tried not to compare her life with Kitty's, but recently Bridie had grown more aware of their differences. Perhaps it was due to her brother Michael's resentful comments or maybe a result of the increasing amount of time they were now spending together; whichever the case, Bridie was being given a bigger window into Kitty's life and a greater perspective, causing her to wonder why it was that Kitty had so much when *she* had so little.

She could hear voices downstairs; her father and brothers playing cards, Mr Hanratty, drunk on his own poteen, snoring loudly from her mother's rocking chair, and the longing in the lyrics of 'Eileen a Roon' sung to the haunting tones of a lone fiddle. It was a comforting and familiar lullaby, and Bridie soon drifted off to sleep.

She awoke abruptly at dawn to the sound of loud knocking on the front door. It was still dark, but for a streak of red bleeding into the eastern sky. The knocking was insistent. She sat up and wondered who would come calling at this time of the morning. At length she heard her father's heavy tread on the stairs and felt a cold sliver of wind, like one of the snakes St Patrick banished from Ireland, winding its way round her door and slipping into the room. She shivered and pulled the blanket tightly around her. A moment later the door slammed and the footsteps went back up the stairs. The house was silent again but for the chewing of a mouse beneath the floorboards under her bed, and the moaning of the wind outside.

'Da, who was at the door this morning?' she asked her father when she came down for breakfast.

'No one,' he replied, taking a loud slurp of tea.

Old Mrs Nagle crossed herself. ''Tis the auld Banshee with the first of three knocks, God save us,' she said darkly. Mrs Doyle blanched and crossed herself as well, sprinkling drops of holy water around the room from the little Norah Lemonade bottle by the door.

''T'was a tinker, more like,' said Sean with a chuckle.

'Whoever it was, he was off before I got to the door,'

Tomas Doyle continued. Bridie cut herself a hunk of soda bread upon which she spread a thick layer of butter. She didn't like the frightened expression on her mother's face and tried not to look at it.

''T'was the Banshee,' said Old Mrs Nagle, crossing herself again.

'Lord preserve us from the Banshee!' muttered Mrs Doyle.

'I tell you, woman, there was no one at the door. Sean's right. It must have been a tinker in search of a warm hearth. Come, let's not be late for Mass.' Her father stood up.

Bridie dismissed dark thoughts of the Banshee, who, as legend had it, was a fairy woman heard wailing when someone was about to die. Well, there had been no wailing, as far as she had heard, so her mother and grandmother were overreacting. As she walked down the street on the way to the school house she saw, to her relief, an old shabby horse pulling a cart full of grubby-faced children. There were skinny goats tethered to the back and one or two young ones inside the cart. The ragged children watched her with wary black eyes as she passed, but the mother was too busy shouting at her husband to even notice her. Tinkers, Bridie thought happily. Her father had been right. They'd probably spent half the night knocking on doors in search of a warm place to sleep. Bridie quickened her step. Her father had told her never to trust a tinker and never to look one in the eye.

The school of Our Lady in Ballinakelly was run by the church but fortunately Father Quinn had little to do with the day-to-day teaching. Bridie's teacher was a nun from Cork City called Sister Hannah who was softly spoken and kind. 'It is through education that we better ourselves,' she had once told Bridie's class. 'The only way out of poverty is through learning, so listen hard to what I'm teaching you. They can take everything you own but no one can take your heart or your mind or your love of God. They're the only things that really matter.' Bridie concentrated hard, but Jack O'Leary, who was in the boys' class next door, just gazed out of the window and watched the birds.

At the end of the day Bridie and Jack found Kitty in her usual place on the wall. However, this time she was standing on one leg, very still, like a heron. 'What are you doing?' Jack asked.

'Balancing,' she replied.

'Why?'

'No reason. For fun, I suppose. It's a challenge. What are you doing?'

'Jack has to give a lesson about birds tomorrow in school,' said Bridie. 'A punishment for gazing out of the window during class.'

'There's no challenge in that,' said Kitty. 'There's nothing Jack doesn't know about plovers and cormorants!'

'Indeed, and I'll give Sister Margaret a lesson she'll never forget.' Jack laughed.

'Doesn't she know you're an expert?' Kitty asked.

'She will tomorrow,' said Bridie, flushing with admiration for Jack.

'Come and balance with me,' Kitty exclaimed. 'It's much harder than it looks. Come on!' Jack scaled the wall like a monkey while Bridie struggled to find her footing. After a while Jack put out his hand and hauled her onto the top.

'Don't you go falling off now,' he said to her and Bridie looked down anxiously.

'I'm not sure I can do it,' she said.

'Course you can. Like this.' And he lifted one foot. 'Easy,' he crowed. 'Now *you* do it.' But just as Bridie was about to raise her leg they heard voices in the trees behind them. Hastily they jumped down, even Bridie who was afraid of heights, and crouched out of sight.

'Who is it?' Jack hissed. 'Did you see anyone?'

Kitty and Jack raised themselves up so they could just see over the wall. There, sneaking in among the trees, was a ragged group of people trespassing on Lord Deverill's land. Jack pulled Kitty down with him. 'Tinkers,' he snarled. 'They were in town this morning.'

'I saw them too,' said Bridie, pleased to be able to add something to the conversation. 'What do they want here?'

'Game,' said Kitty darkly. 'They're after anything they can eat.'

'I'd say they're after more than that. We have to warn Lord Deverill,' said Jack excitedly.

'Follow me,' said Kitty. 'I know a quick way to the castle.'

The three children crept around the edge of the wall until they reached a farm entrance, which was easy to scale.

They scampered eagerly up the dirt track until they reached the stables at the back of the Hunting Lodge.

'What's the matter with you three? Running from the Devil, are you?' asked Mr Mills, who was busy in the stable yard with the horse and trap Lady Deverill had just brought back from her trip into town.

'There are tinkers in the trees,' gasped Kitty, catching her breath.

'They're up to no good, Mr Mills,' Jack added.

'We've come to tell Lord Deverill,' Bridie joined in eagerly.

'Slow down now. Tinkers in the trees, you say?'

'Yes, we must tell Grandpa,' Kitty insisted, hoping her grandfather would get his gun out and fire at them from his dressing-room window.

'No need to bother Lord Deverill,' said Mr Mills. 'I'll get some of the lads and we'll deal with them ourselves. Now where are they?'

'We'll show you,' said Kitty, hopping from foot to foot with excitement. 'Hurry before they get away!'

'Miss Kitty, you'd better stay here. It might be dangerous,' said Mr Mills.

'Then I *must* come!' Kitty exclaimed. 'I'm not afraid of a few tinkers.'

'Your grandfather would not thank me if you came to harm.'

Kitty pouted crossly. 'But I *want* to come.'

'You're safer here,' said Mr Mills firmly and Kitty was

189

left with no alternative but to watch Jack, Bridie and Mr Mills set off towards the wood with Sean Doyle, Bridie's brother, and some of the grooms and beaters, armed with sticks and hurleys.

Bridie felt more courageous with her big brother by her side. Like her father, Sean wasn't tall but he was strong and fearless and deeply loyal to the Deverills. If there was a thief on Lord Deverill's land he'd be sure to see him off and give the man such a fright he'd be unlikely ever to come back. Now they walked through the walled vegetable garden, past Lady Deverill's greenhouses and on out the other side to the paddock where some of the horses grazed lazily in the waning light. This way they came to the wood from the eastern side and worked their way towards where the children had seen the tinkers. It was dark among the trees and the air had turned cold and moist. They crept as quietly as cats, alert to every sound.

Suddenly they came upon them, ragged, unwashed, wild-looking wanderers. The woman carried two pheasants and a partridge by the neck while the men were standing staring into a bush, presumably having spotted something worth poaching. Bridie noticed that one of the pheasants in the woman's grasp looked like it was still alive, twitching every now and then in a vain attempt to escape. She glanced at Jack and saw his face contort with outrage. When the tinkers noticed Mr Mills and his men they swung round and froze to the spot like animals trapped with nowhere to run. There was no point hiding their spoils; they knew they'd been caught red-handed. Two skinny men and one woman were no match for Mr Mills and his burly boys. 'You're trespassing on Lord Deverill's land,' said Mr Mills sternly.

'Lord Deverill's land. Well, we didn't know,' said one of the men, grinning toothlessly.

'I'll kindly ask you to put down those birds and leave at once.' The men narrowed their eyes and looked Mr Mills up and down as if calculating the risks involved in a fight. Sean held up his pitchfork and the look on his face left them in no doubt that they'd be the worse off. They scowled and ordered the woman to drop the birds.

'Curse you!' she screeched at Mr Mills, but he wasn't alarmed by the feeble words of a tinker woman.

'Be off with you now before we call the constabulary and have the three of you locked up,' he said with the authority of a man who has the full weight of Lord Deverill behind him. The woman reluctantly threw the birds to the ground and the three of them slowly walked away.

Mr Mills patted Jack on the head. 'Good stuff, lad,' he said. 'And Bridie, where would she be got to?' Mr Mills searched through the semi-dark for Bridie. When he saw her cowering behind her brother he nodded his appreciation. 'You too, Bridie. I will tell Lord Deverill. I'm sure he will want to reward you.' Bridie's eyes widened and she caught Jack's eye. 'Now be off with you, too, before it gets too dark to see the end of your nose.'

The night was drawing in, bringing with it bitterly cold winds. Jack and Bridie made their way back to Ballinakelly with a skip in their step. They had had quite an adventure and looked forward to a generous reward from Lord Deverill. When they reached the town they were horrified to find themselves face to face with the tinkers, preparing their horses for departure. Glancing about them they saw the street was quiet, except for the golden light inside O'Donovan's public house opposite. Seeing the children the tinker woman pointed at them accusingly and shouted something in a dialect that neither Jack nor Bridie understood. Before Jack could register what was happening he felt a blow to his jaw and fell backwards in the mud as one of the men dealt him the full might of his fist. Bridie let out a scream, so loud and piercing that the pub door opened, throwing light across the place where Jack lay inert. A moment later Bridie's father Tomas hurled himself into the street. Just as one of the tinkers pulled back his arm to give Bridie a similar blow, Tomas grabbed him by the shoulder and thumped him on the nose. Blood spouted from the tinker's face and he recoiled, landing on his backside in the mud. But the other man came at Tomas from behind and he had a knife. With one thrust he dug the blade through Tomas's ribs.

Somewhere deep in the woods came the distant shriek of the Banshee, carried on the fairy wind that had suddenly risen.

Songs of Love and War

Santa Montefiore

Their lives were mapped out ahead of them. But love and war will change everything ...

West Cork, Ireland, 1900. The year marks the start of a new century, and the birth of three very different women: Kitty Deverill, the flame-haired Anglo-Irish daughter of the castle, Bridie Doyle, the daughter of the Irish cook and Celia Deverill, Kitty's flamboyant English cousin.

Together they grow up in the dreamy grounds of the family's grand estate, Castle Deverill. Yet their peaceful way of life is threatened when Ireland's struggle for independence reaches their isolated part of the country.

A bastion of British supremacy, the castle itself is in danger of destruction as the war closes in around it, and Kitty, in love with the rebel Jack O'Leary and enflamed by her own sense of patriotism, is torn between loyalty to her Anglo-Irish family and her deep love of Ireland and Jack...

HB ISBN 978-1-47113-584-2
EBOOK ISBN 978-1-47113-587-3

FIND OUT
MORE ABOUT
SANTA MONTEFIORE

Santa Montefiore is the author of
twelve sweeping novels.

To find out more about her and
her writing, visit her website at

www.santamontefiore.com

Sign up for Santa's newsletter and keep
up to date with all her news.

Or connect with her on Facebook at

http://www.facebook.com/santa.montefiore